The

Elizabeth Pewsey was born in Chile to a South American mother and an English father – her Argentinian grandmother was a poet and, she says, 'as nutty as a fruitcake'! Both parents were writers and great travellers, and she lived in India as a child before the family settled in Britain, where she finished her schooling and went to Oxford University. She now lives in Somerset with her husband and two children.

The Walled City

ELIZABETH PEWSEY

Dolphin Paperbacks

For Rachel Carberry
who likes dragons

The other books in the trilogy
The Talking Head
The Dewstone Quest

First published in Great Britain in 1998
as a Dolphin paperback
by Orion Children's Books
a division of the Orion Publishing Group Ltd
Orion House
5 Upper St Martin's Lane
London WC2H 9EA

A catalogue record for this book
is available from the British Library

Typeset by Deltatype Ltd, Birkenhead, Merseyside
Printed in Great Britain by Clays Ltd, St Ives plc.

ISBN 1 85881 306 9 (pb)

One

THE TALL, DARK MAN AND THE GIRL WERE THERE again.

The first time, they had stopped her in the street. They were holding a map, but they didn't look lost.

He wasn't the kind of man to be lost, Scarlet had thought, as she directed them to a bank.

Then she'd run into the girl in the library. She had smiled, but Scarlet wasn't impressed. She didn't look like a girl who smiled a lot. Fit, though, Scarlet knew about muscles and sinews, and she had plenty of those. And an American accent, judging from their brief conversation.

'Hi.'

'Hello.' Coldly.

'Do you know where the reference section is?'

Scarlet had pointed silently to an arrow on the wall and a sign above it which said 'Reference Library'.

The man joined the girl a few minutes later. Scarlet, mooching through some magazines, could hear snatches of their conversation from behind the dictionaries. They were father and daughter, Scarlet decided. They were very alike; not to look at, but in their expressions, and in the air of extreme competence they both had.

Scarlet opened another magazine at random, ears pinned back. What on earth were they talking about?

Vemoria, that must be some place in America she'd never heard of. And they were taking someone back when they went. Poor them, thought Scarlet, growing bored with eavesdropping and wandering off to the talking books section.

Two days later, a car had drawn up alongside her as she was walking home from school. It was the man again, with the girl beside him. They smiled at Scarlet. 'Hi,' said the girl. 'Can we give you a lift?'

For all the friendly smiles, the message came over loud and clear, don't mess with us.

'No, thanks,' said Scarlet. 'I don't want a lift. I'm meeting a friend.'

Then it happened.

Like in your worst dreams, or nightly on the TV. As Scarlet walked away, the car followed her, creeping along the kerb just behind her.

She quickened her pace. So did the car.

She slowed down. Guess what, she told herself, they're after me. When the street is empty, as it could be, any minute, one or other or both of them are going to hop out and drag me into the car.

Not without a fight, she thought, tensing her muscles for a sprint.

Waste of time. She couldn't outrun a car.

Use her karate training?

Not against two of them, and those two in particular, with their lean, mean physiques.

Forget it.

Juggler Street was a long, straight street, with boarded-up shops and garages, all shut and offering no refuge. On the other side of the road, where there was no pavement, was a high brick wall; beyond that,

Scarlet knew, a steep embankment led down to the main line of the railway.

Her mother had said she shouldn't walk back from school that way. 'Too lonely,' she insisted. Her mother was thinking of some of the town's livelier spirits who roamed free out of school hours, and in them, too.

Scarlet knew that her mother would never have imagined this strange pair in the black car dogging her footsteps.

In desperation she increased her speed, almost running now, and skidded to a halt beside a door set into the wall between a workshop and another closed garage. It must have been a grander area once, and this stout wooden doorway set in a pointed, brick arch was a relic of those more prosperous times. Scarlet had given it a push once or twice on her way home, out of curiosity. It had always remained firmly shut.

So why should today be any different?

Scarlet wasn't thinking logically, so she didn't tell herself the door would be locked as usual.

And it wasn't. As she hurled herself against it, it swung open and she tumbled through. Then, quick as a flash, and still without thinking, she picked herself up, slammed the door shut and shot a huge bolt across. Then she leant against the door, eyes shut, listening to the furious hammer blows and yells coming from the other side.

Two

THE BANGING FROM THE OTHER SIDE OF THE door grew fainter and fainter, as though either Scarlet or the man and girl were vanishing into the distance.

Scarlet opened her eyes, expecting to find herself in an overgrown yard, and, given her luck this afternoon, probably a yard with no way out except back through the door.

Where she actually found herself was in a very narrow, sloping street, full of sunlight. There were houses on either side of her, built of pale stone, narrow and about three storeys high. The windows had flowers growing in boxes on the sills. Some of the houses had tiny balconies, and these too were full of flowers.

Scarlet put out a hand and touched the stone, warm in the sun.

Feeling hotter and hotter, she looked up and down the deserted street. At the bottom there were three steps, and beyond that she could see another narrow street at right angles to this one.

The heat was overwhelming and inexplicable. When she had gone through the door, it had been a drizzling, grey, chilly December afternoon.

She had emerged into this brilliant sunlight and the kind of warmth you might have on a day in high summer, if you were lucky and it was an exceptionally good summer. Summers where Scarlet came from tended to be wet and mild, not sunny and hot.

Scarlet shut her eyes, shaking her head as though to shake the sight of the street and the warmth away, and then opened them again.

The street was still there.

So was the heat.

Well, she might be dreaming, but she was still going to take off her coat. And her blazer. And for good measure she yanked off her school tie and stuffed it into her pocket. School rules were firm on the subject of ties; full school uniform had to be worn on the journey to and from school. Scarlet wasn't a good rule-keeper at the best of times, and this present time was so strange that she wasn't going to bother about a tie.

Somehow, she felt, neither Mr Dunster nor Miss Millican nor any other of the school staff were about to come round the corner and give her a detention.

Feeling less hot, but still perplexed, she headed for the steps and the other street. It was slightly wider than the one she had come down, and not as steep, but otherwise it was very much the same.

Scarlet paused, thinking hard. There was nothing to be gained by staying there, she needed to find out where she was, and she wouldn't do that if rooted to the spot. On the other hand, the door she had come through was in the steep, narrow street, and that might be the only way back to known territory. If she set out to explore, would she be able to find her way back?

Scarlet knew her limitations. It was no use trying to keep a tally of left and right turns. Left and right were a mystery to Scarlet, as were dates and numbers and a few other useful things. So she'd have to remember landmarks. If only the front doors and the houses weren't so similar. If only the streets had names.

Reading didn't come easily to Scarlet, either, but she was okay, mostly, with street names.

If these streets had names, then they were some place where she couldn't see them. Well, she could leave her coat down there, where the corner of a house jutted out slightly from the next one. Nobody would take a coat, not in this weather, she told herself as she rolled her coat and blazer into a bundle. There. She'd notice that when she came back, and know that the door was in the street leading off from there.

Scarlet looked up and down the wider street. She could see a patch of green, or at least a tree at one end of it. If nothing more, it would be a shady place to sit and work out what she was going to do.

That was another odd thing. It was about four o'clock in the afternoon, growing dark on a winter's afternoon. A glance at her watch showed the time, ten to four. Yet the sun was shining brilliantly, at its zenith, beating straight down so that even the narrow streets gave no shade.

Very odd indeed, Scarlet thought. Still, no point in standing around like a lemon. Move, she told herself.

That was a strange doorway, set in a stone surround with barley-sugar columns. She'd remember that. And the bright blue front door a few houses along. Maybe the streets weren't all as samey as they had seemed at first.

As she got nearer, Scarlet saw that the green patch and the tree was more than that, it was a tiny square. And the tree, which did indeed give shade, grew to one side of a fountain, where water was tumbling out of the raised mouth of some strange bird-like creature.

Very unusual, in Scarlet's opinion, but it made a change from the normal dolphins and lions' heads.

The fountain had a small wall round it, at a

convenient height for sitting on. So Scarlet sat, and listened to the splashing water, and watched the pattern of the leaves, and wondered where on earth she was, and what she was going to do next.

'Nowhere on earth,' said a loud voice, startling her out of her wits.

She looked around. There was no one to be seen. The voice must have come from one of the houses round the square, but how? All the windows were shuttered against the blazing sun. Was she imagining things?

'On the other hand, somewhere not on earth,' said the voice, finishing its unhelpful pronouncement with a harsh cackling sound.

The voice came from above her. Definitely. Scarlet peered up into the branches; someone must have climbed the tree.

'Not necessarily,' said the voice, and with a few rustles and creaks a black shape dropped out of the tree and landed beside Scarlet. It shook its feathers and stretched out first one large claw and then the other.

'You're a bird,' cried Scarlet. 'A talking bird.'

More harsh cackles, this time sounding indignant. 'I am not a bird,' it said. 'No, not a bird,' it repeated. Or did it? Was it the same voice, or were there two voices speaking? Scarlet looked up into the tree, and then looked back at the bird.

She looked, and blinked, and then looked again. 'You've got two heads,' she said finally, taking in the full glory of the golden beaks and the two fierce heads with huge golden eyes.

'Why not? I'm an arpad, and we arpads have two heads. Haven't you ever seen one before? Or at least a picture? It's very rude to stare, you know.'

'On the other hand, maybe not,' said the other head. 'She may be full of admiration for our fine looks.'

Scarlet agreed about the looks, because the bird, which was nearly half her height, and with a lustrous blue-black sheen to its feathers, was indeed a fine sight. Still, she found the two heads hard to take.

She was about to speak to the strange creature when she heard the sound of running footsteps.

Panic.

It had to be them, the sinister pair who had been after her in Juggler Street. They must have got through the door after all. At least here, in this unfamiliar place with its narrow, enclosed streets, she might have a better chance of getting away from them.

Oh, help, she thought. Who were the two of them, and what did they want?

Three

SCARLET TENSED HERSELF FOR A FAST START, flashing a look over her shoulder before making a dash for it.

Then she stopped, stood quite still, relaxing her clenched fists, letting her breath go. This wasn't the man or the girl, but someone quite different. A boy of about her own age, with hair a lighter red than hers and the bluest eyes she'd ever seen.

'Hi,' he said to her, at the same time sketching a bow towards the arpad.

'Hi,' said Scarlet. 'Why did you do that?'

'Do what?'

'Bow. To the bird.'

'It isn't a bird,' the boy said after a moment's thought. 'It's an arpad, and you have to bow, they're sacred.'

'Oh,' said Scarlet.

'You don't often get close to them,' said the boy. 'Just as well, because they're quick with their beaks, come at you with a fast one, two, and that's you with slashes all over you.'

'Oh,' said Scarlet again, looking at the arpad with increased respect. 'It can talk.'

'*She* can talk,' said the arpad, sounding annoyed. 'We are she.'

'Definitely she,' agreed the second head.

'She'll have a name,' the boy confided to Scarlet in a whisper, 'but you mustn't ask. It's terribly rude to ask. You must be new here, or you'd know. Have you skived off school?'

'No,' said Scarlet. 'School's finished, it finished . . .' She looked at her watch. Ten to four. Still ten to four? She gave her wrist a good shake, but the hands stayed motionless; her watch must have stopped. 'I don't know what time it is, but school ended at least half an hour ago.'

'Sounds unlikely to me,' said the boy. 'My school goes on for another hour until lunch, and then back for more this evening. Have you got evening school?'

'Evening school?' What a terrible idea. 'No. Are you skiving?'

'Yes,' said the boy, plonking himself down by the fountain, at a careful distance from the arpad, who was busy pluming herself. He dabbled his fingers in the water. 'It was so boring, and it's so warm outside. I just sloped off.'

'They'll notice you've gone,' said the arpad, putting both heads out of her feathers to speak.

'Or maybe not, if all the others are concentrating on their lessons,' pointed out the other head.

'They'll notice,' said the boy with a sigh. 'They always do, that's what comes of being tuned in to all those different dimensions and so on.' He took his hand out of the water and dried it on the tunic he was wearing. Then he held it up. 'I'm Pebin.'

'Scarlet.'

'Are you a soothsayer, too?'

'A what?'

'Obviously not.' He looked at her with new interest. 'Why are you wearing those clothes? Are you from the Gonelands? Or from the Third Lands, perhaps?'

'I don't know what you're talking about. I came through a door from Juggler Street, and I live in England, and I haven't a clue where I am.'

Four

'IS THAT ARPAD, OR WHATEVER IT'S CALLED, going to stay with us?' Scarlet asked in a low voice. It certainly seemed to be following them, walking on its big claws in a stately way, both its heads keen-eyed and noticing everything. 'It gives me the creeps.'

Pebin nodded. 'I've never been this close to one. Usually they despise people and keep their distance. There's nothing you can do about it, no one would dare question what an arpad does.'

They were on their way to Pebin's house. 'One of my brothers may be in,' said Pebin. 'Or will be soon. They'll know where you've come from, I should think. They're up on that kind of thing.' He turned down another street, wider this time, which had a shallow channel running down the centre.

'Is that a drain?' asked Scarlet, thinking of mediaeval sewage systems, and wondering if a window was going to be opened above her head and something unspeakable flung out over her.

'No, it's for cleaning the streets. They turn on the pumps and send water through whatever part of the city the street cleaners are working on. We're fairly low here, and it comes down with a rush, you get wet feet if you aren't careful.' He stopped in front of a wide, dark red door. 'This is my house.'

'Oh!' said Scarlet, looking around in amazement as

she stepped through the door. The walls of a big entrance hall were covered in tiny mosaic squares, which shone and glinted in endless, shifting colours. 'It's lovely. I've never seen a house like this.'

'No one is in, by the sound of it,' said Pebin, sliding his bag across the floor and leading the way through an arch into a square yard. The arpad followed, its claws clicking on the smooth stone floor.

The yard was enclosed on all sides by the house, with windows opening out into the central area. Plants twined round the pillars and along the gallery at first-floor level; the strangest plants Scarlet had ever seen, with broad purple leaves and bright red flowers the size of saucers. A staircase led up to the first floor, and Scarlet counted six doors, all shut, tucked away behind a colonnade of stout pillars. 'Wow,' she said. 'Some place.'

Pebin shrugged. 'This? It's very plain and basic. My parents are keen on the simple life.'

'Simple! You should see the houses where I come from,' said Scarlet, thinking of her own tidy clone of a house, identical to dozens of others on the estate, each with a tiny garden and patch of grass in front.

Pebin frowned. 'You must surely be a Tuan, whatever you say. Are you from the south?'

'I'm not a Tuan, whatever that is,' said Scarlet.

'I never knew anyone but Tuans to have red hair like yours.'

'Yours is red, too.'

'Yes, but lighter. And I am a Tuan.'

Scarlet felt tired and hot and thirsty. And confused. 'Can I have a glass of water? And then I want to know where I am and how I got here and how I get back.'

'And why she's here,' put in the arpad. 'The why is always important in these matters.'

'Quite,' agreed its other head. 'If anyone knows, that is.'

Pebin had vanished, to return with a glass of water. No ordinary glass, Scarlet noticed, taking the heavy blue and grey goblet. Inside, the colours swirled round into a kind of whirlpool at the base.

'Like an optical illusion,' said Scarlet. 'It makes me feel odd, looking down into it.'

'Soothsayer's glass,' said one arpad head.

'This is a soothsayer's house,' said its twin. 'You can see visions in those glasses.'

'Or not, depending on who you are.'

'It's very hot here,' said Scarlet. 'Can we go inside?'

'Outside's cooler,' said Pebin. 'We'll go into the garden.'

The garden was full of more strange plants, several of them with huge leaves, an arm's spread across, which hung overhead and provided patches of dappled shade.

Pebin propped up what seemed to be a dull-surfaced mirror against the central stem of one of the plants.

The arpad croaked approval from both beaks.

'What's that?' asked Scarlet.

'You want to know where you are, so I'll show you,' said Pebin. 'Only before I do that I want to know where you come from.'

'Bit difficult to explain,' said Scarlet. 'I live near London.'

'Oh?' said Pebin.

'You have heard of London?'

'No.'

'Oh. Well, you've heard of England?'

The arpad gave a caw. 'England. Otherworld, continent of Asia.'

'Wrong, wrong,' said the other head. 'Europe.'

'Yes, Europe,' said Scarlet. She didn't like the sound of this.

'It doesn't mean very much to me, Europe,' said Pebin.

'Don't break your brain on it. Now, I've told you where I've come from; you tell me where I am.'

'You're in the Walled City, which is in the northern part of Tuan.'

'Tuan's a country, and you're a Tuan?'

'Yes. The Walled City is very old and very special, since it's where you learn magic. I live here, because both my parents work here, and they teach as well. Mostly, people come here to study and then go away.'

'Like a university city?'

'If you say so.'

'I've never heard of it.'

'Doesn't exist where you've come from.'

A loud caw. 'It does.'

'Doesn't.'

'I tell you, it does.'

Just now, the argumentative arpad was more than Scarlet could stand. 'Shut up!' she shouted.

'Well, really,' said one head, affronted.

For once, the twin head was in agreement. 'Really, indeed. You try to help, and get shouted at.'

'Just give me some space,' said Scarlet, sitting down on a pale blue bench. 'Where on earth am I?'

'That's it,' said Pebin. 'Not exactly on earth at all. Our world and your world – and lots of other worlds – touch, so they say.'

'Who says?'

'People who've come through from the Otherworld. They come through for some reason, for a purpose. That's what I was told.'

'I haven't come here for anything I know about,' said

— 15 —

Scarlet. 'I've only got your word for it that this is a different world from mine. Maybe I believe you; this isn't like anywhere I've ever been.'

'People come through when there's something only they can do here.'

Scarlet was scornful. 'How could that possibly be so in my case?'

'I'm just telling you what people say.'

'People say anything.' Scarlet thought for a moment, tempted by the idea of staying for a while in this strange place, but deciding against it. 'The best plan is, we go back to that door I came through, and I just slip back into my own world. I reckon it's a case of mistaken identity, And there's probably someone with a purpose, like you said, on the other side longing to come here.'

'I doubt it,' said Pebin.

'Not exactly busloads of tourists coming this way, then?'

'Tourists?'

'Oh, forget it. Tuan, did you say?'

'I'll show you,' offered Pebin. 'If you're going back, you might like to know where you've been.'

'Mind patterns,' said the arpad.

'Mind *maps*,' said number two.

'Same thing.'

'Not at all.'

Pebin took no notice of the bickering bird, but laid the mirror flat on the ground.

Scarlet gazed down at it. 'It looks as though it's liquid.'

'Go on looking.'

Scarlet didn't need encouragement; it was utterly fascinating. As she stared and stared, lines formed on the dark surface; lines which twisted and turned and joined together.

'It's a map!' said Scarlet.

'Yes.'

'A map of here?'

'Of here and hereabouts.' Pebin spoke in a toneless voice. And he didn't look at Scarlet or at the arpad. He had a blank expression, as though he was focusing his eyes on something which no one else could see. 'It may not be accurate, not in detail,' he went on in the same flat voice. 'I'm not very good at this yet.'

'Are you doing that with your *mind*?'

'Of course he is,' said the arpad. 'Hard work.'

The other head flicked its beak upwards in contempt. 'Easy-peasy when you know how.'

Five

'THIS IS TUAN,' SAID PEBIN, POINTING.
    'North Tuan,' said Beak One.
'Obviously,' said Two.
Pebin took no notice of the interruption.
'This country in the middle is Vemoria.'
Here the beaks were in agreement, for once, and the
big bird gave a shake that made all her feathers fluff out
before they settled back into their usual shining smooth-
ness.
    'Vemoria,' said One.
'Horrible place,' agreed Two.
'I've never been there,' said Pebin. 'I know about it,
though. It's ruled by a group called the Twelve. They
took over from the Old Kings, and well, kind of tidied it
up.'
    'Tidied it up!' Beak One was indignant.
'They're control freaks, those Vemorians,' said Two.
'That's what everyone says,' said Pebin. 'Everything
is very rigid. They love water, and have canals everywhere, they go by canal instead of on roads. Even in the
cities, their main streets are canals.'
    'Like Venice,' said Scarlet, who had never been there,
but had seen a film set there. 'Great.' She thought of the
graceful sweep of the Grand Canal, with the sunlight
sparkling on the water.

'Not like that at all,' said Pebin. 'In Vemoria, all the canals are absolutely straight.'

'How do you know what I'm thinking?'

'Just a knack,' said Pebin and went quickly on with his geography lesson. 'This is the border between us and the Third Lands, and the Land of the Gods,' Pebin continued.

'The *what*?'

'Third Lands and Land of the Gods.'

'And the inhabitants there are who? No, don't tell me. Gods.'

'Gods and Immortals.'

Was she dreaming? It was the obvious explanation to Scarlet, but if so, how could she wake herself up?

And it didn't feel like a dream. There was a reality to the sunlight coming through the leaves, to the warm dusty smell of the air as Pebin scuffed the ground with a sandalled foot, to the arpad having a quick preen with both her beaks. For a moment, she panicked, what if she was here for good? Lost, out of time. Then she flicked the horrors away. She had come through a door from Juggler Street; very well, then she would be able to go back through a door into Juggler Street.

Pebin was back in Tuan now, pointing his finger at the western part of North Tuan. 'This is where we are. The Walled City.'

'Why is it walled? Who's going to attack it?'

'They aren't those sort of walls, they aren't battlements and so on. It's walled because there are walls everywhere. The houses form a wall, and then at the back they all have high walls. Like here.'

Scarlet looked at the end wall, which was three times her height. 'What's the other side of the wall?'

'A narrow street, more an alleyway, really. Then more walls.'

'Very secretive.'

'No secrets here,' said Pebin. 'The place is full of soothsayers and clairvoyants and mind-readers and all sorts.'

'Jeez,' said Scarlet, with feeling. 'So how do you get to be good at all these psychic tricks?'

'Tricks?' said Beak One.

'They are tricks,' said Two.

'Rubbish.'

'Rubbish yourself.'

'We Tuans are like that,' said Pebin. 'We always have been. Everybody has some skills, and if you're really good, then you get sent here, to learn in the Walled City.'

'Is that what you're doing?'

'Um,' said Pebin, shifting from one foot to the other. 'Not exactly. My parents are especially good at it all, you see, they both come from families who've always produced very powerful soothsayers and so on. That's why they live here. And it's kind of taken for granted that all of us – me and my brothers and sisters – are going to be the same. So we get the training whether we want it or not.'

'And are you all good at it?'

'Not me,' said Pebin. He looked uncomfortable. 'I just don't seem to be able to get it together, not like the others . . .' His voice trailed into silence.

Scarlet shrugged. 'So? I'm pretty bad at reading, and letters and so on. It doesn't bother me. Or it does,' she added honestly, 'but you get used to it. I can do maths okay, and I understand things really quickly, so I get by.'

'You aren't a Tuan,' said Pebin. 'I don't expect your parents nag at you about why you aren't doing better.'

'Parent,' Scarlet corrected him. 'I've only got one parent, my mum. And she nags, they all do.'

'Father dead?' asked Beak One with interest.

'Don't be nosy,' said Two.

'Not as far as I know,' said Scarlet. 'He and my mum split up. He got married again, I think. I never see him, and he's never tried to see me.' She stretched and yawned. 'That's why I've got to get back. Mum'll be worried about me if I'm not home from school on time.'

'All right,' said Pebin. 'We need to find that street with the door you came through.'

'I left my coat at the corner of it,' said Scarlet. 'If we can find that, then I can just go up the street, through the door, and back where I came from.'

'It doesn't always work like that,' said Pebin, 'but we can try.'

The arpad stretched her wings, making Scarlet skip smartly out of the way. She looked at the big bird with new respect; not many birds had a wingspan the width of a garage door.

'We will do a reconnaissance flight,' said Beak One grandly.

'We?' said Two. 'How about consulting me first?'

'You going to refuse?'

'No.'

'Stop moaning, then.'

The arpad stretched up on to the tips of her giant claws and with a loud flap of its wings was on top of the wall. 'Back soon,' said Beak One.

'Maybe,' said Two, as she swooped up into the sky.

Scarlet craned her neck as the bird made a sharp banking turn and soared out of sight. 'Will it come back?' she asked Pebin.

'You never know with an arpad,' said Pebin.

'Actually, I've never exchanged two words with one before.'

'Two words is right,' said Scarlet.

Pebin looked at her, and then laughed. 'Yes, they are a bit argumentative, aren't they. I just wonder why she's turned up. Out of my league, a bird like that. Usually, they hang around with the types up at the castle.'

'Castle? I thought you said this place wasn't built to repel attackers.'

'True, so I don't know why there's a castle. But there is. It's very old, and it sprawls over about a third of the city. It's like a mini-city itself, with passages and little courtyards, fountains, stairways, great underground halls, towers, pools. Easy to get lost there.'

'Easy for me to get lost anywhere,' said Scarlet.

Six

PEBIN AND THE BIRD SEEMED QUITE SURE ABOUT where they were going.

Scarlet wasn't convinced. 'I don't remember this at all. And I only went a short way until I met you, and then it wasn't far to your house. I'm sure it must be nearer than this.'

The arpad, yomping along on its big claws, disagreed.

'Distances are deceptive,' said Beak One.

'It isn't distances which are deceptive, it's our perception of distance which is at fault.'

'Speak for yourself, there's nothing faulty about my perception.'

I wonder if they ever actually peck each other. Scarlet eyed the curved golden beaks. Not possible, she decided, and then wondered if the arpad could mind-read as well. Those unblinking eyes were very unnerving.

At last, here was the fountain. With the tree, throwing its shadow further round than before. Scarlet had no idea of the time, and of course her watch, even if it hadn't stopped, would be wrong for this place.

'Past noon,' said Pebin. 'This is where we met, by the juniper tree.'

'Only that peacock wasn't there then,' said One, snapping its beak shut.

Beak Two squinted at the fountain. 'Dimwit,' it said. 'Idiotic bird.'

The peacock let out an eerie peacock's cry and hopped up from the edge of the fountain into the tree.

'Funny,' said Pebin. 'Something's up. A sociable arpad, and now a peacock at the fountain. And the weather's changing.'

Scarlet looked up into the sky. 'Looks the same to me.'

'Getting hotter,' said Pebin. 'Can't you feel it? And it's heavy.'

'Heavy weather?' said Beak One. 'Sounds impossible.'

'Why not?' said Beak Two at once. 'Light weather this morning, heavy weather this afternoon.'

Beak One turned its mind to more important matters. 'I saw clothing down there.'

Scarlet looked where the claw was pointing. Was that the way she had come? She thought not, but then, she couldn't be sure.

'You saw?' Beak Two didn't like that at all. 'We saw, if you don't mind. You always assume you've spotted something first, and in fact, my eyesight is better than yours.'

'Since when?'

'Since always.'

'This way, then,' said Pebin hastily.

'There,' said both beaks together. 'On the corner.'

'That's not my coat,' said Scarlet at once. It didn't look like anyone's coat, more like a pile of old sheets.

'There's something under it,' said Pebin, stepping back. 'It's moving.'

'Rat!' cried the arpad, lunging.

There was a loud and non-ratty shriek as the bundle of sheeting took on human form and flailed vigorously with its arms against the vicious beaks. 'Get off,' a voice cried.

'Not a rat,' said Beak One, disgruntled.

'*I* never thought it was,' said Two.

'What is it?' whispered Scarlet, as the figure wound itself into a kind of spiral and then unwound to stand upright.

'It's a man,' said Pebin, who was staring hard. 'But a very strange one.'

'It's rude to stare,' said the figure.

He swayed as he spoke, as though he were a dancer, thought Scarlet. He unfurled himself from his wrapping, and stood before them in a tunic like Pebin's, only reaching to the ground.

'Are you all right?' asked Pebin.

'No, since you ask,' said the figure.

'Who are you?'

'Ivar, at your service.' He gave a stately bow, and toppled over, landing in a strange heap, as though he had collapsed in on himself.

'There *is* something the matter with him,' said Scarlet.

'Sorry about that,' said Ivar, getting to his feet again. 'I'm not used to this, and it takes a lot of effort.'

'What does?'

'Standing. Walking. Sitting. All the usual things.'

'Why?'

Ivar didn't answer Pebin directly, but instead asked him a question. 'Are you a local? Do you live in the Walled City?'

'Maybe,' said Pebin.

'Happen to have seen any bones?'

'Bones? Whose bones?'

'Mine.'

Seven

PROPPED AGAINST THE JUNIPER TREE, IVAR
told them about his missing bones. How he had got
on the wrong side of a friend – friend? wondered
Scarlet – who had taken his revenge by removing his
bones and spiriting them away to an unknown place.

'I wouldn't mind quite so much if they'd left me a
few to be going on with, but oh, no, it had to be the
whole lot, nothing less than my skeleton would do.'

'Who is they?' asked Scarlet. 'And how on earth did
they take your bones out? It must have been agony.'

'No,' said Ivar, rather crossly. 'They, that is this
friend and a crony of his, did it while I was asleep.
Magic, you know, they didn't actually hack into me, in
case you wondered.'

Pebin seemed to take all this for granted. Scarlet
didn't believe a word of it. But nonetheless this guy was
either boneless or had rubber bones. Which is ridiculous, Scarlet told herself firmly.

'It's that mob in the Land of the Gods,' said Ivar,
pouting. 'They're completely out of control. So
unfriendly, and quite unnecessary to do this to me. I
only played a tiny joke on Ril, ages ago. It wasn't my
fault that it got him on the wrong side of one of the
Gods.'

'Bad news, that,' said the arpad.

'I know it isn't very pleasant to lose your head, but

after all, he did get his body back in the end, and no harm done.'

'Lose his head?' Scarlet shook her own head. 'What is all this?'

'It happens,' said Pebin. 'Typical punishment or penance for getting on the wrong side of a God, although there's usually more to it than that. And I've heard about Ril's head.'

'So have we,' said the arpad, nodding both heads with great vigour.

'All we Tuans know the story,' said Pebin. 'Ril is an Immortal. He had to come and fight for the Tuans when the Vemorians attacked us a while back. Once the battle was over, he had to have his head cut off. There weren't many Tuans about to decapitate him, and they argued about it, and nobody wanted to do it. Luckily, two Otherworlders had come through, and they did the dirty work on his neck.'

'They cut his head off? Was he dead?'

'Not exactly, being an Immortal. It was gory, but not cruel, he wouldn't have *felt* it exactly. Then the two Otherworlders carried the head across Vemoria and buried it on the hill outside the Walled City, beyond the East Gate. That restored our lost magical powers, and meant we were able to settle matters with Vemoria.'

He gave Scarlet a calculating look. 'And now here's Ivar the Boneless, just when you've come through from another world.'

'A coincidence,' said Scarlet quickly.

'The two Otherworlders were called Gilly and Hal. Do you have names like that?'

'Sure,' said Scarlet. 'Where did they come from?'

'A country called England.'

'Yup, that's the same place I come from. Did they get back?'

'Yes, once they'd done what they had to.'

'Like what?'

'The head.'

'Ah.'

'They came back again, after that,' put in Beak One.

'Yes,' said Pebin. 'To help the boy with red hair to find the Dewstone.'

'Red hair?' said Scarlet.

'Yes, just your colour,' said Two.

'Coincidence,' said One.

'Maybe,' said Beak Two.

Scarlet wanted to know what a Dewstone was. Pebin, the arpad heads and Ivar all spoke at once, and she was none the wiser when they had finished. 'A stone of power? Oh, come on.'

'No, really,' said Pebin. 'Dewstones are very ancient and powerful. The red-headed boy was the only one who could find this one, Dewstones are like that. Mind you, he didn't keep it. He threw it deep into a gorge when he found out what its powers were. Too dangerous to handle, he thought, and he was probably right.'

'You said he came through from my world,' Scarlet said, her mind on essentials. 'How did they get back. Through a door?'

'I don't know,' said Pebin.

'Mist,' said head One. 'They came through the mist.'

'They went *back* through the mist.'

'Came and went, then,' said Ivar, whose attention was on other matters. 'I'm so glad they helped Ril get together with his head, and I only wish they were around to find my skeleton for me.'

'Perhaps that's why you're here,' Pebin said to Scarlet.

'What, to go hunting for bones? No way. Besides,

Ivar must have bones. If he hasn't got any bones, how can he stand up?'

'Willpower,' said Ivar with a sigh. 'It's very tiring.'

'Look, I sympathize, okay? I think it's pretty careless to go losing your skeleton, but it's nothing to do with me.'

'What is to do with you?'

'Getting out of this place,' said Scarlet firmly. 'I reckon I go back the way I came. I saw that blue door when I came here. I just need to find a street with a few steps, a steep one, and halfway along there'll be a door, and I'll be back in a rainy old Juggler Street.'

'Maybe' said Two.

'Most unlikely,' said One.

'Goodbye then,' said Scarlet. 'Nice to have met you, if I have. And I'll think of you, hunting for your inner frame,' she said to Ivar. 'It'll liven up biology no end, thinking I've met a guy without any bones.'

'So long,' said Pebin.

'Goodbye,' said Scarlet, and set off down the street.

Eight

SHE WAS RIGHT.

There was her coat. She hesitated for just a second before taking it out from behind the doorstep where she had lodged it. Her coat wasn't likely to turn out to be a person with no bones, but in this place, who could tell?

She went quickly up the steps, and along the narrow alleyway. There was the balcony with the particularly bright flowers, so the door must be over there.

House with a blue door, house with a red door. Another red door and then a blue door. Lots of doors. Each clearly attached to a house. No doors set in the wall, not one.

Must have got it wrong, thought Scarlet. It must be further up.

Further up were more houses and more doors. None of them in the least like the door she had come through. She kept going; perhaps she had forgotten a turning.

There were no turnings, and the street didn't lead anywhere. It simply ended, abruptly, with a high wall.

Missed it, thought Scarlet, retracing her footsteps.

She stopped by the second red door. She was sure the door she had come through had been here. Perhaps she'd got the colour wrong. This must be it.

What if it wasn't? What if she pushed at it, and it opened, and she was in someone's house?

So what? she told herself. In that case, she'd just say

sorry and shift herself back on to the street. But it wouldn't happen. She'd open the door, and she'd be back in Juggler Street. Late home, of course; her mother would be cross, no going out on Saturday night.

Scarlet didn't mind. Scarlet felt that staying at home might be a good idea, if you could get caught up in this kind of a fix when you went out.

She gave the door a push.

Nothing happened, so this time she tried a good shove. The door opened instantly and smoothly, and she was inside before she could see what was there. Thank goodness, she thought. She'd picked the right one, it was dark, and much colder. She was back where she belonged.

Nine

*I*T WAS UTTERLY DARK.

Strange, because even on the darkest nights, when there was no moon and the skies were heavy with rain, Scarlet's home town had a glow to it. There were the lights from the road on the other side of the railway, what had happened to them? And what about the lights from the houses in the street, which you should see even from this side of the road? Where were they?

There was no light at all.

And then Scarlet wondered if she was actually outside. It was impossible to tell in the darkness, but she just felt enclosed.

No good standing about like a wally. She wasn't afraid of the dark, never had been. On the other hand, she didn't remember it ever being as dark as this.

Too bad. She took a deep breath, started humming her favourite tune, and edged forward.

Clunk.

Slap into a wall. Scarlet recoiled, rubbing her shoulder. Okay, so not that way. Try another direction.

Clunk. That was her other shoulder.

She turned extremely slowly, very deliberately placing her feet so that she would be able to judge just how far round she had gone.

Another bruise to her shoulder, and then another one.

This was very strange. Upwards? Could she be in a shaft?

A nasty thunk on her knuckles told her that she wasn't.

Right, Scarlet said to herself. I've ended up in the coal cellar. Pretty stupid to have a coal cellar painted red and leading on to a street like a front door, but then this is a stupid place. Still, no need to panic. She just had to feel round and about until she found the door. A door that led in would also lead out.

Not so.

There was no door. Scarlet was in a black chamber, hardly bigger than she was, with no light and no way out.

Oh well, thought Scarlet, as she slid down to sit on the cold ground with her hands wrapped round her knees. I know where I am all right now. This is a nightmare. A Class A nightmare, a spooky special. So all I have to do is wait until I wake up.

In which case, she thought, wishing it weren't quite so cold, she might as well shut her eyes and be asleep properly.

But what if she didn't wake up? If the sunlit world of the Walled City wasn't a dream, then this wasn't a nightmare. Scarlet didn't want to think about that. No, she would force herself to be asleep, to stop the panicky thoughts flying round inside her head, to forget the darkness and the not knowing where she was. So she shut her eyes, not that it made any difference, and settled down to wait for something to happen.

She must have drifted off to sleep, because she was woken – minutes or hours later, it was impossible to judge – by an eerie, scraping, metallic sound, and a bright light which shone down from above her head and almost blinded her after the inky blackness of her sleep.

The chamber wasn't solid, as she had thought, for above her there was a grid, now pulled to one side. A face peered down at her, a round face with big dark eyes. A woman's face.

'Dear oh dear oh dear oh dear,' it said, in a wheezy voice. 'Whateverhavewegot here oh dear oh dear.'

Her words threaded into each other in the oddest way; just my luck, thought Scarlet. I wake up from my nightmare part one, and find I've got to the comic bits.

Which, she knew from experience, are often the worst part of a nightmare.

'Nightmare? Oh no oh no oh no, nonightmare, notatall, oh dear oh dear.'

Surprisingly, Scarlet found that her courage and optimism were rising. If this isn't a nightmare, she told herself, then I'm about to meet someone quite out of the ordinary, by the sound of it. A nutter, obviously.

'Nutter? Nonononononono.'

The words floated down to Scarlet, who felt that, even if like so many others in this weird world the woman could read her mind, it was better to speak.

'Let me out,' she said clearly.

'Letyououtletheroutletthecaptiveout.'

This was hopeless. Scarlet spoke more slowly. 'I'm cold, and uncomfortable, and I don't know why I'm here. And I'd like you to get me out.'

'Getherout, getherout, getherout.'

Blooming madwoman. Just her luck. 'Can't you fetch help?'

'Helphelp, oh dear oh dear oh dear.'

Was that getting through to her? 'Yes, HELP!'

'No need to shout,' said the woman calmly and

—— 34 ——

perfectly clearly. 'Of course I can help. Shut your eyes, think of nothing, and you'll be out of there in a trice.'

That was a problem. How do you think of nothing?

'You'd better find out, or you could be down there a long time.'

Oh, very helpful.

'Make your mind a blank.'

Easy to say, hard to do. The more Scarlet tried, the more thoughts came tumbling into her head.

'Stop trying.'

'Oh shut up, you old bag,' said Scarlet, exasperated, and let go, and then . . .

. . . Suddenly . . . her mind was as empty and black as the space around her had been . . .

. . . and the woman was holding a hand down and she was whizzing up into the air as light as a feather.

'Which you aren't,' said the round-faced woman, looking at her.

'No,' agreed Scarlet, still struggling to get her breath back. She sat up, and breathed in and out like someone just come out from under the waves. 'Wow.'

'Cup of tea?' asked the woman. She held out a brown, plump hand. 'I'm Natar.'

'Scarlet.'

'You'd better have some sugar in your tea. I dare say it was a shock, finding yourself in that place.'

'Yes,' said Scarlet. 'Although I just seem to go from place to place, and each one is stranger than the one before, and all I want to do is go home.'

'Oh, I don't think you can do that just yet,' said Natar, handing her a delicate cup and saucer full of a dark and fragrant liquid which didn't look like any tea Scarlet had ever had.

Tea, how uncool.

'Quite,' said Natar. 'Hot, in fact. It'll do you good, bring your sense back, if you've got any.'

'Oh, thanks,' said Scarlet.

She sipped at the noxious brew, which actually turned out to be drinkable. Different, and Scarlet wasn't going to make a habit of it, but it was okay in the circumstances. As she drank it, she looked at her new surroundings. The large woman with the moon-face looked like a hippy, but her room didn't go with her at all. No shabby furniture and heaps of this and that.

Not at all.

'I'm a minimalist,' said Natar, following Scarlet's eyes as she took in the glass table, the bare polished floor, the plain and uncurtained windows. There were sitting-on benches which also seemed to be made of glass. Tough on the bum, thought Scarlet, apart from being so slippery.

'Made of glass, yesglass glasssssss . . .'

She's off again, thought Scarlet, and indeed she was. Natar's head fell to one side, her eyes closed . . .

Scarlet felt a surge of indignation. Her rescuer had fallen asleep. Just like that. Now what was she supposed to do. Explore?

Not a good idea. Scarlet had already noticed the square grids at intervals in the gleaming floor, and she had an idea that they might all belong to little cells like the one she'd been in. Glass or no glass, she'd rather be up here, with this snoring loony, than back down in the darkness.

Those black globes over there on a glass shelf. What were they? They looked as though they might be of the night sky, with little pinpricks of light showing through. But the patterns didn't look like the ones she was used to – and where was the light coming from? There were no wires visible.

Batteries? Scarlet thought not, batteries and Natar didn't seem to go together. And it was a moving light, the little sparkles coming and going. And the light changed colour, look, now the glowing points were red.

Scarlet liked the look of those, she wouldn't mind having one of them in her room at home. She had a lava lamp that an aunt had given her, and she used to watch it for hours. She wished she was at home now, looking at her lamp. Yes, she was adventurous, liked new things, enjoyed change.

Within reason.

And all this, Scarlet knew for certain, was way outside any reason.

Ten

'NOT A NUTTER, NO, NO,' SAID NATAR, WAKING up with a start that sent her sliding along her seat. She braked with her shapeless feet, yawned widely, and then turned her attention to Scarlet.

Those eyes weren't brown. They were black. No, that wasn't right, either. Black was flat; Natar's eyes were like a tunnel of darkness. So like a tunnel that you could almost feel you were being drawn into them . . .

'Hey! Stop that!' said Scarlet, alarmed.

'Not too sure about being hypnotised, is that it?' said Natar.

'I'm quite sure about it, thank you. I don't want to be hypnotized, not by you or anyone else.'

'You may not always have a choice,' said Natar. 'And I nearly got you then.'

'Well, you didn't. Nearly isn't enough. And while we're on the subject of hypnosis and suchlike, why do you keep falling asleep?'

'I don't.'

'You do. You did it just now. And you were half asleep when you opened up that grid.'

'Not asleep. Watching. A very different matter.'

'Watching? Watching what?'

'Vemoria, mostly.'

Scarlet grew more alert, as a memory stirred. Where had she heard that name? Not only since she came to the Walled City, but before. In the library, that was it, when she had eavesdropped on that tall man, and the girl. She had heard them mention Vemoria.

Why had they been talking about Vemoria? If it was in another world, then why should they? No, she must have misheard. What had Pebin said? Canals, that was it.

Natar nodded. 'Canals, yes. And the Twelve. Do you know about the Twelve?'

'Nope. Only what P... what someone told me. Twelve people rule the place or something like that.'

'Twelve did, one does.'

What was that supposed to mean?

'That's why I'm watching a lot. Quite a lot of trouble over the border there, yes, trouble indeed. One of the Twelve has ideas above his station. Uthar, he's called. He's got rid of the other eleven rulers and taken over by himself. He has a daughter called Erica.'

'So?'

'Erica's half an Otherworlder. Her mother comes from your world.'

'How do you know where I come from?'

'Oh, I know a lot of things. Do you know anyone called Erica?'

'As it happens, I don't.'

'Not even heard of one?'

'There was one at our school for three weeks. I never met her, right, because I had mumps, I was off school.'

'What was she like? Did your friends say?'

'I don't see that it's any of your business, but they said she was a real cow, so I don't mind telling you. She was American, or Canadian, from somewhere like that. Apparently, she was good at everything schools like you to be good at: games, English, languages, science, maths. "Well done, Erica, top in this, top in that, Head's Commendation, Erica.'"

'Nauseating.'

'She was. But she didn't win any prizes with any of my friends, because she was a freak. Cold as ice, always expected people to do what she told them, ugh!'

Scarlet remembered the buzz about the girl when she got back to school. She hadn't believed what people were saying about her; she had thought they were making it up to shock her. She had left a taint behind her, too, old friends had become distant, people were wary of each other, tempers were short.

'And did they?'

'Did they what?'

'Do what she told them?'

'Now you come to mention it, they mostly did, yes. They said it was as if she'd controlled them, made them do what she wanted. She'd even asked questions about me, which was a cheek, apart from being a bit creepy.'

'What sort of questions?'

'Oh, was there a girl at school with flaming red hair, why wasn't I at school, where did I live, who were my parents, all that kind of thing. Dead nosy.'

'She sounds it.'

'Why are you asking all these questions? The Erica where I come from isn't likely to be this Uthar's daughter, is she? There must be thousands of Ericas.'

'She might be.'

'Not very likely.' Scarlet shifted along her seat. 'Listen, thank you for the tea, and for getting me out of that place, but I think I should be off now.'

'Where to?'

'I'm looking for a door which will take me back where I came from.'

'I can direct you there.'

Scarlet waited; Natar said nothing. Then she got up and went to the window furthest away from them. 'Did you look out of here while I was watching?'

While you were asleep, Scarlet amended under her breath. 'No. I thought I might disappear down through one of your grid affairs, and be back where I started.'

'Very wise. Come and look.'

Scarlet had to admit that the view from the window was astonishing. 'How come we're so high up? I mean, I went through a door on the ground floor, and this can only be one floor up from that.'

'It doesn't work like that. This is a tower.'

'A watchtower,' said Scarlet. 'Since you're a Watcher.'

'Exactly.'

'Is that the castle?' asked Scarlet, her attention caught by a high wall running round a tightly packed collection of roofs and towers.

'Yes.'

Scarlet looked down at the rest of the town. They were way above the city, and she could see the streets laid out as though she were looking at an aerial photo. 'All those high walls,' she said. 'And so many gardens and fountains.'

'We need the fountains; it gets very hot in summer, and the running water helps to cool the air.'

'Fine,' said Scarlet. 'So where's the door I need to go through, and how did I get to miss it?'

'Passing doors never stay in the same place.'

Scarlet stared at her. *Here we go again, more nonsense. What's wrong with these types?* she wondered.

'Was the arpad nonsense?'

'Weird, should be in a zoo.'

'And Pebin's mind map?'

'How do you know about that? I never said anything about Pebin.'

'No. Good, you'll need to keep your mouth shut.'

'What's the point, when people read your mind?' Scarlet hadn't mentioned this before, but it was beginning to irritate her, as she told Natar.

Natar laughed, a deep and jolly laugh. 'Not everyone can do that. It takes skill and training, you know. Lots can in the Walled City, it's one of our specialities, but you won't find it a common habit elsewhere.'

'I had noticed,' said Scarlet. 'Okay, how do I find this door?'

'The door's there, somewhere, but I think it may be difficult to find. I expect you've come through to do something. Most do, you see, and it will be easier for you to go back once you've found out why you're here.'

'No thanks,' said Scarlet. 'I'd rather just go back, however difficult it is. And I don't believe I'm here to do anything. It's just a mistake.'

'I think not,' said Natar. 'There's trouble stirring, and I'm sure you're meant to help.'

Natar didn't wait for Scarlet to answer, but instead looked across the room at the black globes.

Scarlet couldn't believe her eyes. The door, Juggler Street, tasks were all forgotten as the globes began to move, apparently of their own accord. They floated at first just above the shelf, and then drifted out into the room to hover at about eyelevel. They twinkled as they turned slowly round, and they seemed to have misty patches trailing across their surfaces.

'How do they do that?' Scarlet was impressed, despite herself. 'They're lovely. Do they have batteries?'

'No, we have no batteries in this world. And they don't do it, I do.'

'You? How?'

'With my mind.' A flick of her eyebrows, and all of them except one, the smallest, went back to the shelf, each one dropping neatly down, still twinkling.

'You can do it, too. Possibly.'

'Do what?'

'Use your mind. These work on directions from your mind.'

Now she'd heard everything.

'Let your mind go blank. Stretch out with your mind and let it hold the ball. Try it.'

That was the globe, lights out, at her feet. It rolled along the floor, and then stopped. An ordinary black ball.

'I've broken it,' said Scarlet, looking down at the plain dark ball. 'My mind couldn't hold it. It was stupid to try.'

'No, you haven't broken it.' Natar flashed a look at the ball, and it sparkled upwards again. 'Go on, keep it there.'

The ball landed on the floor with a thud this time, and Natar floated it up into the air again.

And again.

And again.

Scarlet was getting cross; this was an absurd waste of time. She could see that there was something thoroughly mysterious about the globes, and she could tell that Natar was able to float and move this one. But not her, she didn't have a clue how to begin.

'Reach out for it,' Natar said once more. 'Let your mind float, and think the ball along.'

What a waste of time this was, when all she wanted was to get away. On the other hand, if Natar could do it, why couldn't she?

And then, just for a fraction of a second, she felt her

mind gather itself, focus, and the ball stayed up for a tiny moment before it crashed down on to the floor.

'There,' said Natar. 'Told you so. You can do it. Keep trying, keeptryingtryingtrying . . .'

Bother her, off again. No more sense out of her until she came round again. Meanwhile, had she really held that globe with her mind, kept it twinkling? She could just have a few more goes, see if she could lift it off the floor.

Her eyes were on the one on the floor, but her mind flicked over to the shelf. And before she knew what was happening, one of the much bigger globes had risen into the air and was starting a series of wild swoops and zigzags about the room.

I'm doing it, thought Scarlet. That's me.

It was the strangest sensation, a tingling at the back of her head, a slight pain in her eyes. She tried to get the globe to slow down, to float in a more peaceful way, but if anything it became faster and wilder in its movements.

Scarlet ducked as it came straight for her. It missed her by a whisker; 'I'm not sure this is a good idea,' said Scarlet, struggling to loosen her mind's hold. A memory of the hated Erica flashed into her head, the tingling stopped, the globe landed with a loud crash on the floor, and Natar came to with a startled yelp and a gigantic yawn.

'I did it,' said Scarlet smugly.

'So you did,' said Natar.

Eleven

SCARLET HAD GONE OVER TO THE ROUND window and stared down at the streets again.

'There are your friends,' Natar said. 'Pebin and the arpad.'

'And Ivar, look, he's collapsed in a heap. It must be very exhausting, having no bones.'

Scarlet wondered about the little group by the fountain, under the juniper tree. The peacock was still there with them. 'They're looking a bit jumpy.'

'Everyone in the Walled City is starting to look a bit jumpy.'

'Why?'

'I told you, there's a smell of trouble in the air. Stand back, I'm going to summon Pebin, and the arpad.'

With a whistling noise, one of the medium-sized black globes whizzed past Scarlet's ear and shot through the glass of the window as though it were water. For a second or two it hovered in midair, and then it launched itself downwards and cruised along the streets towards the little group by the fountain.

Even before it reached them, Pebin had jumped to his feet and was pointing at the flying ball. The globe swung itself round the juniper tree, hovered for a few seconds, and then set off on its way back, gliding in front of Pebin, who was running, and the arpad, who had taken to the air.

The globe came back to Natar with a thin shriek and sank back on to the shelf. Natar hastily opened the window with a snap of her fingers, just in time for the arpad to sail in and land with a scrunch of claws on the floor.

'Scratching the polish,' grumbled Natar.

Footsteps sounded outside the door. Natar made a clicking sound, and the door swung open to show Pebin with his hand just raised to knock.

'Hi,' he said to Scarlet. 'Thought you'd gone.'

'I keep trying,' said Scarlet.

'Summoned by a thoughtball,' said Pebin. 'That's a first. Were you controlling it?' he asked Natar.

'I was.'

'Pretty good.'

'Unlike you, young Pebin, playing truant from your classes again today, were you?'

Pebin looked uneasy. 'Um,' he began.

'You'll never make a soothsayer that way.'

'I'll never make a soothsayer any way,' said Pebin, who didn't sound bothered at the thought.

'There are other skills.'

'Not ones that I've got.' Pebin looked round the room, his eyes bright with interest. 'Why are we here? Why did you summon us? How did Scarlet get here? And why . . .?'

'I'll tell you, skill-less boy. I'm a Watcher, as you know. I watch Vemoria especially. Now, I'm going to send a thoughtball to Vemoria, and I want you to draw what it sends back.'

'Huh?' said Scarlet.

Natar kept on looking at Pebin.

'Mind drawing,' he said. 'I can do that. Anybody can do that.'

'I hear you're especially good at it. The skill you deny you have. I want you to draw a face!'

Pebin considered for a moment. 'A face? That's difficult.'

'Try. Have you heard that the Twelve have fallen?'

A look of alarm flitted across Pebin's face, and Scarlet could see that he had clenched his fists. 'Only rumours. Have the Old Kings come back?'

'No.'

'Phew.'

Scarlet wanted to know more. Old kings sounded intriguing, even if they were worrying Pebin. 'Who are the Old Kings?'

'They ruled Vemoria before the Twelve. They were strong magicians, full of the old wild magic. Modern Vemorians are rational, and can't use magic.'

'Unlike Tuans.' Pebin spoke with pride.

'Magic can get you into trouble,' said Beak One. Both heads kept their golden eyes on the thoughtballs as they spoke.

'Not if it's used wisely.'

'Nothing wise about the Tuans.'

'It's worked,' Beak One pointed out. 'The Vemorians use their soldiers and reason and force. The Tuans fend them off and protect their borders by their skills at soothsaying and clairvoyance and far-seeing.'

Scarlet thought that sounded an unequal contest.

'There's a balance,' said Natar, twitching her broad nose as though a fly had landed on it. 'Bring back the wild magic, and the balance is upset.'

'*Can* Uthar bring back the old magic?' Pebin asked.

'The Old Kings are gone, none are left, and the wizards and sorcerers were all banished.' Beak One was definite.

Beak Two knew better than that. 'One was left. One

descendant, and he was young, he might now have children of his own.'

'True,' said Natar. 'And if Uthar can get hold of the descendant of the Old King, then there's trouble for all of us.'

'Pity the Dewstone's at the bottom of the Spellbound Gorge,' said Beak One.

'Just as well,' said Beak Two.

The Dewstone again. Scarlet was longing to know more about this Dewstone, but the information that it was a stone of power, with which Uthar could do a lot of no good, left her none the wiser than after Pebin had first told her about it. This annoyed her, it was obvious that the Dewstone was important and she still wasn't sure why.

'You'll find out soon enough,' said Natar unhelpfully. 'Now, we haven't got much time. I need to send the thoughtball. Pebin, sit over there, by yourself. Silence, now.'

'Caw,' said Beak Two.

'Shut up,' said One.

Twelve

'WHAT'S HE DOING?' SAID SCARLET IN A whisper. 'Who's he drawing?'

Pebin was sitting, tense, hunched up on one of the glass seats, his hands over his face. His whole attention was focused on the wall opposite. A panel of darkened glass was attached to this, and on it he was drawing, as he had the maps. Only this time it was a figure.

The body was a shadowy outline, but he was starting to fill in the details, seeming to gather colours from the dark glass and lay them down like a painter.

'He's seeing through the thoughtball,' said Beak One.

'Seeing *with* the thoughtball,' corrected Two.

'You mean the thoughtball is somewhere else, hovering near this person, and Pebin can see it?'

'In this case,' said Natar, 'the thoughtball is near a picture, not looking at the actual person.'

'A picture of a picture, then.' Scarlet shifted on her seat. For some reason the figure Pebin was working on made her feel uncomfortable. Ridiculous; she couldn't even tell yet whether it was a man or a woman.

'Man,' said Natar.

'Red-headed,' said Beak One, turning its head away from the shelf of black globes for a moment and looking straight at Scarlet. She wriggled under the direct golden gaze.

Not even Two could disagree; the man in Pebin's picture had flaming red hair.

'Like yours,' said Two, blinking at Scarlet. 'Just like yours.'

'Plenty of people have red hair,' said Scarlet.

Eyes, hooded, wary, giving nothing away. A long nose, a firm mouth; Pebin was nearly done.

And he was exhausted. The last details were filled in slowly and hesitantly, and then he toppled sideways and slid in a heap on to the floor.

'What have you done to him?' said Scarlet, leaping up.

'He'll be all right,' said Natar. She pointed to the picture, which was still clear on the wall. 'Have a good look. A really good look, because it'll fade soon. That's the trouble with using someone half-trained, like Pebin here.'

Fade, would it? Good, the sooner the better. Scarlet didn't like the look of the man in the picture at all; he gave her the shudders. Funny, because he didn't look like Dracula or the man at the newsagent with the terrible squint. She just didn't like him; he made her feel uneasy.

How stupid, it was just a picture of a stranger. And yet, he was familiar. Had she ever met him? Had she seen a picture of him before? Not very likely, unless he came from her world.

'Who is he?' she asked.

'You don't know?'

'If I knew, I wouldn't ask.'

'He's a prisoner,' said Natar.

'What did he do?'

'Do?'

'Yes, why is he in jail? Burglary? Fraud? Murder?'

'Not that kind of prisoner.'

'Oh. What kind, then?'

'Prisoner of war, I think you'd call him.'

'Is that why he has a hunted look? Because he's a prisoner?'

'Perhaps. Also, he has heavy responsibilities, and has had to take impossible decisions.'

'Why are you showing us this picture?'

'Then you'll know who he is when you find him.'

'I'm not going to find him.'

'I think you are.'

Thirteen

*I*VAR AND THE PEACOCK WEREN´T GETTING ALONG too well, and he was relieved when a small boy arrived in the square and announced he'd come for the creature.

'What a dim bird,' said Ivar. 'Can't think why you bothered to come and get it, I'd have left it in the juniper tree.'

'He's not an it, he's a him,' said the boy. 'And I'd be really stupid if I left him up the juniper tree, this is one valuable bird.'

'Valuable to who?'

'To me. I breed peacocks and sell them.'

Ivar raised his eyebrows. 'You should be at school.'

The boy gave him a contemptuous look. 'I look after the peacocks when I've finished at school.' Then he frowned. 'What's wrong with you? Why are you all droopy?'

'I've lost my bones,' said Ivar morosely.

'*All* of them?'

'Yes.'

'I know where there are some bones. Maybe they're yours.'

'Where?'

'Come with me and I'll show you. It's on my way home.'

The boy tucked the grumbling peacock firmly under

one arm, and stalked off, not waiting to see if Ivar was coming with him.

'Listen,' said Ivar, catching up with him. 'About these bones. Where did you see them? How long have they been there?'

'If you didn't talk so much, we'd go faster.'

'You aren't taking me to a graveyard, are you?'

'Graveyard? That's disgusting. I'm not a grave robber.'

'If my bones were there, and I got them back, then it wouldn't be robbery.'

'Suppose not.' The boy made an abrupt right turn. Ivar wasn't quick enough and ended up wrapped round a pillar on the corner.

'Cool!' said the boy admiringly. 'I don't know why you want your bones back.'

'Take it from me, I do.'

'Nearly there.'

They had reached a livelier part of the city. Shops were opening up after the midday break, people were coming and going, stopping to gossip to friends. And, as always in the Walled City, there were sorcerers and soothsayers and clairvoyants.

'You can tell them by the faraway look in their eyes,' Ivar's guide said. 'Dafties, they are.'

He turned into a dark, narrow street, away from the bustle, and stopped outside a shop.

'Here you are,' he said.

The peacock looked in at the dark and gloomy window and let out a discontented shriek.

'He's hungry,' said the boy. 'Hope the bones fit.'

'Hey,' said Ivar, but the boy had gone. Ivar peered into the shop window, but could see nothing. He stepped back and looked at the fascia. Written in flowing letters were the words *Skulls, bones and skeletons.*

A bone shop? He'd never heard of such a thing. Suspicious, he took a deep breath, composed his wonky limbs and pushed open the shop door.

Fourteen

'OUCH,' SAID PEBIN, SITTING UP AND RUBBING his eyes. 'My head hurts.'

'It would,' said Natar. 'Lack of experience. As you do more of it, you'll find you get used to it, and your head won't hurt so much.'

'More of it?' said Pebin, alarmed. 'No thank you.'

'Oh, you will,' said Natar. 'You're a natural.'

'Did I see anything? Did I draw it?'

'Him,' said Scarlet. 'A man with red hair. Don't you remember?'

'No,' said Pebin.

Natar made a clicking noise with her tongue. 'Now, that's a nuisance,' she said with a frown. 'It would be much better for both of you to know what he looked like.'

'Why?'

'Safety in numbers,' said Natar. 'I told you, you need to recognize the man in the picture. Now, where's that arpad?'

Scarlet looked round the room in surprise. 'It was here just a minute ago, going on about red hair. There you are, the arpad saw the picture, another identifier, if you need one. Or two.'

'Arpads are unreliable.'

'Not at all,' said two croaky voices at once, as the arpad landed at their feet.

'Where have you been?' said Natar.

'Looking for Ivar.'

'Did you find him.'

'Yes,' said Beak One.

'Good,' said Natar.

'Bad,' said Two. 'He was going into a house just off Glim Square.'

'Not . . .'

The two heads nodded violently. 'Querle's house,' said One.

'Are you sure?'

'Yes,' said Two.

Fifteen

'WHO'S QUERLE?'
   'Gatekeeper,' said Pebin, panting.

'How's your head?' said Scarlet, who was running easily alongside him, while the arpad hopped and flapped a little way behind.

'Awful,' said Pebin.

'I don't know why I'm doing this,' said Scarlet, as Pebin dived off into yet another street. 'What a maze this is.'

'Quite,' pant, 'straightforward,' said Pebin. 'Compared to the castle.' He slowed to a walking pace. 'Stitch. And my head's going to fall off.'

'No, it isn't,' said Beak One.

'It might,' said Two. 'People do lose their heads.'

'Not in the street in broad daylight,' said One loftily.

'How can you be so sure?' Pebin turned into a narrow, dark street. 'Is this it?' he asked the arpad.

'At the other end,' said Two.

'Near the square,' added One.

Pebin set off again.

'Gone,' said One.

'The shop's gone,' agreed Two. 'It was here.'

'This flower shop?' said Pebin. A small woman with an innocent face was spraying a bucketful of handsome red spiky flowers which were standing among an array of similar containers set out on the street.

Scarlet peered into the shop window. It was full of plants, many of them brightly coloured and exotic-looking; all of them unfamiliar. There was a small tree, as well, and some birds hopping about in cages.

'What kind of a shop was it?' asked Pebin. 'When you saw Ivar go in?'

'It said Bones and Skeletons across the top.'

'It says Walled City Blooms now.'

'You can see why he went in.'

'How can a shop have changed between when you saw Ivar and now?' said Scarlet.

'Same reason as that door you keep on about isn't where it was when you came through it,' said Pebin. 'These entrances and exits tend to move around. Castle ones, especially.'

'Does it matter?' said Scarlet. 'Isn't Ivar just as likely or unlikely to find his bones in the castle as anywhere else?'

'You don't understand,' said Pebin. 'The castle isn't like the rest of the Walled City. It's much older, for one thing, and there's some very weird magic goes on in there for another. I've never been in the castle. Most people haven't.'

'Doesn't look to me as though you're going to go in there now,' said Scarlet, looking at the flower shop. 'Best leave Ivar to his own devices. I don't see why we've got to help him to meet up with his skeleton in any case. Really, it's none of our business.'

Scarlet knew better than to meddle in other people's business. At her school, it was best to know only what you had to. And then, with a stepfather like hers, you learned to keep your head down, and your thoughts to yourself.

'Crook, is he?' asked Pebin.

'No,' said Scarlet, although she wasn't too sure. 'He just likes to get the better of people.'

'Do you get on all right with him?'

'No. I can't stand him, and he loathes me. The upshot is, my mum has turns. She longs for us all to be one happy family, but it isn't going to happen.'

'You could always find your own father.'

'I might, if he'd ever wanted to see me. For all I know, he isn't even aware that I exist; he walked out before I was born.'

'Sad,' said Two.

'A challenge,' said One.

'Hell,' said Pebin, pushing himself off the wall against which he had been leaning.

'So, what now?' said Scarlet. She felt in her pocket, reassured by the smooth feel of the thoughtball which Natar had given her.

She hadn't wanted it at the time.

'Take it,' Natar had said, barring her way out. 'With it you can follow Ivar. And Ivar knows where the man with red hair is kept prisoner.'

'Why does he know that? I don't think he knows anything, his mind is full of lost bones. And even if he does know, so what?'

'You must find the prisoner, before Uthar does.'

'You're crazy. This is nothing to do with me.'

'It has. Believe me, it has. That's why you're here. Help Ivar with his bones. Then, in return, he'll tell you where the prisoner is. That's the way back to your world.'

'Tosh.'

'You haven't found your doorway yet. And Pebin needs your help.'

'No, he doesn't.'

'He does. You can use the thoughtball, he can't.'

And how come I can? Scarlet wondered. And what use would her feeble efforts in that direction be?

'You were born with the skill. When you really need to use it, you'll find you can.'

Scarlet looked unhappily round the room, almost wishing that Natar hadn't hauled her up out of the black hole. She wasn't going to give in, she wouldn't let herself be nagged like this, even though she did have a sneaking feeling that the prisoner was in some way connected to her and to her own world. 'Meanwhile, my mum's ringing the police and my photo's on the late news.'

'Time on earth isn't the same as time here. The time on your watch is the time in your world.'

'My watch has stopped.'

'When you go back, no time will have passed in your world.'

'No?'

'None at all.'

'And here?'

'I can't say. Hours, days, weeks. As long as is necessary.'

'Necessary for what?'

'Necessary to find the last of the Old Kings. Necessary to save this city and Tuan and Vemoria from the terror of the old, wild magic.'

Old, wild magic, thought Scarlet as she followed Pebin into the square. Old, wild hokum, more like.

Sixteen

QUERLE WAS A TALL, MEAN, LEAN INDIVIDUAL. He took his gatekeeper duties seriously, and was known throughout the castle as Old Misery. His hair was long and grey and straggly, he had a wart on his nose, and his little eyes were mud-coloured and full of suspicion.

Just my luck, thought Ivar. Seven gatekeepers, and I have to get Querle.

'No question of your coming in, of course,' said Querle, who liked nothing better than to keep people out.

'I'm an Immortal,' said Ivar, collapsing in a neat spiral on the ground. 'You can't keep me out.'

'A deformed Immortal,' said Querle. 'And I can. No rules about Immortals here; I can let you in, or keep you out, as I choose. And I choose not to let you in. I wish you hadn't done that, it makes me feel quite ill.'

'That's nothing,' said Ivar, slithering to a chair and wrapping himself round it. 'It's amazing what you can do when you're boneless.'

'Ugh.'

'I'll make a bargain,' said Ivar. 'You tell me where my bones are, and I'll be off and out of your hair.'

'I don't know where your bones are.'

'They're in here, otherwise there wouldn't have been that shop sign, enticing me.'

Querle's thin mouth gave a nervous twitch. 'There wasn't a shop sign. You imagined it.'

'I didn't.' From his strange position Ivar was watching Querle closely. 'You're lying, look at that twitch.'

'Twitch? What twitch?'

By a great effort of willpower, Querle managed to stop his mouth twitching, only to find that he had an uncontrollable tick in his eye.

'That one.'

More effort, which transferred the nervous tick to Querle's left foot. He glowered at Ivar, trying to keep his foot hidden under the table.

The gatekeeper's lodge, one of seven which guarded the seven castle gates, was in a round tower. The table at which Querle sat was round, too, and the chairs drawn up to the table and set against the wall had curved backs.

Wonder if he's got a round bed, Ivar thought. Or twisted, to match his twisted soul. Come to think of it, a round bed would do for him, the way he was at present, curse Ril and his tricky revenge.

He wound his arms into an elaborate bow. Quite pleasing, in its way, but it didn't have the same impact as folded arms. He leant back in his chair, and stared at Querle.

Querle curled his lip, showing an ugly yellow tooth. Querle knew where his bones were. Querle was an old friend of Ril's. More fool he for putting out the shop front to tease Ivar. If he didn't know about Ivar's search for his bones, why bother to do that? And if he did, then it was because he'd helped Ril to hide them.

But Querle wasn't telling. He was no magician himself, had no skills at all in that direction, but he knew how to keep his mouth shut. That's why the gatekeepers were chosen to do their job.

Ivar unwound himself. 'I'll be on my way, then.'

'Exit's that way,' said Querle, with a jerk of his head.

'So I see,' said Ivar. 'Did you know that there's an enormous spider lowering itself on to your head?'

Querle snarled. 'You won't catch me with an old one like that.'

At which point he felt hairy legs digging into his scalp. He let out a yell, and danced across the room, wrestling with quite the biggest spider Ivar had ever seen.

Not that Ivar stayed around to say hello and talk about the weather. Instead, he shot through the door opposite to the Way Out, ran across the no-man's-land yard outside the door, and through the inner wall into the castle proper.

Where Querle couldn't follow him. Gatekeepers were outsiders, and had to stay outside. There would be other guards inside, and they'd be after him if Querle raised the alarm, but for the time being, Ivar was where he wanted to be, unnoticed and un-pursued.

'Where are we going?' said Scarlet, as they crossed the square.

'We're going to look for another entrance to the castle.'

'An entrance which also shifts about?'

'They mostly do,' admitted Pebin. 'So they say. I don't know, because most citizens don't go into the castle.'

'So we wander about until we see an entrance? Like the door I want to find.'

'No,' said the arpad, both beaks in unison. 'We'll take to the air,' said Beak One.

'Or walk,' said Two.

'Reconnaissance.'

Scarlet sat herself firmly down on a bench. She was hot and sticky and thirsty and tired. 'I'm sorry, but gateways don't move about. I mean, that castle's solid. I saw it from up there. Walls are walls, and gateways are gateways. Walls and gates don't shift from one place to another.'

'No,' said Pebin, 'but each gateway has several doors, and it's a question of whether you can find an open one. Querle opened a door to let Ivar in, and then it closed.'

'Why did this Querle character let Ivar into the castle?'

'He probably didn't,' said One.

'Almost certainly not,' said Two.

'Knowing Querle, he'd take him into the gatehouse, tease him, taunt him, and then send him out through another door. That's what Querle does,' said One.

'If you're lucky,' said Two. 'They say there's an oubliette just the other side of the gatehouse. People drop through it and are never seen again.'

'What's an oubliette?' said Scarlet.

'A forget-you,' said Pebin. 'Hole in the ground, whoosh down into the moat.'

'There isn't a moat.'

'Underground river; the outcome's the same.'

'It all seems a long way from soothsaying and clairvoyance and so on,' said Scarlet. 'Why is the castle so tough?'

'It's old, and it's neutral,' said Pebin. 'It's where the great magicians and sorcerers live. They don't care about Tuans or Vemorians or anything very much. They're supposed to help the Gods keep a balance, but they get obsessed with what they're doing, and end up not bothering very much about what's going on in the outside world.'

'Very unsatisfactory,' said Two.

'It works,' said One. 'More or less.'

We should be able to find Ivar, Scarlet told herself. If he's been tossed out by the Querle character, then the arpad should spot him. He's conspicuous enough, all that waving and wobbling.

Then we have to persuade him to tell us where the prisoner is. Then we find said prisoner and release him; how, no one bothers to say. Then this Uthar guy can't get hold of him, so he stays a small-time pest of a leader instead of a great and powerful ruler with designs on Tuan. And I get to go home.

Fat chance, thought Scarlet glumly.

Seventeen

*I*VAR HAD VANISHED.

The arpad combed the city from the air, while Pebin led Scarlet through street after street. He stopped to ask people if they'd seen Ivar. Instantly recognizable, he told them, a tall man with a bendy body. Shopkeepers, youngsters of Pebin's and Scarlet's age; older teenagers, cool and uninterested; citizens who knew Pebin and his family; they all pursed their lips, whistled, looked thoughtful and shook their heads.

'No, thank goodness,' said one snappy woman, shovelling ice on to fish which lay in gleaming piles on a marble slab. She tipped a stream of golden prawns out into a glass dish, and thumped the bucket down with a crash. 'Sounds a nasty creature.'

'He's an Immortal,' said Pebin.

'They're the worst,' she said, and Pebin jumped out of reach as she nearly landed him a quick one with a large and hideous fish she had pulled out of the display.

Pebin bought little pastries for himself and Scarlet from a stall further down the street; the woman there hadn't seen Ivar, either. 'No, dearies, not today. Saw a strange man yesterday, but he had all his bones as far as I could tell.'

Scarlet enjoyed the hot flaky pastry interleaved with cheese.

'It isn't much,' said Pebin, 'but I'm broke.'

'I've got some money,' said Scarlet. 'Only I don't suppose it would be any use here.'

They had perched on a low wall which ran round yet another fountain to eat their pastries. There was no tree shading them here, but the sun had moved round, and the tall buildings round the tiny square cast welcome shadows.

Scarlet looked up into the deep blue sky, shading her eyes against the sun. 'No sign of the arpad,' she said. 'I think it's buzzed off.'

'It'll be back,' said Pebin. 'It seems to be quite keen to help.'

'Why don't we use the thoughtball?' said Scarlet. 'I know I'm not much good at it, but we could try. Send it to find Ivar, and then follow it.'

'We'd lose it out here,' said Pebin. 'You haven't had that much practice, and it'd just disappear. I don't think it's what Natar meant when she said about using it when you really needed to.'

There was a flurry of wings, and a snap of a beak as the arpad landed, taking a peck at Pebin's pastry as it folded up its immense wings.

'Get off,' said Pebin, stuffing the remains of his food quickly into his mouth.

'I fear,' said Beak One, 'that our boneless friend has somehow managed to stay in the castle.'

'Must have,' said Two. 'No sign of him at all.'

'Well then, it's quite simple,' said Pebin, after a long pause. 'We have to get inside the castle ourselves.'

'Can't,' said the arpad.

'Not unless we can find another gate,' said Beak Two.

'If we could find Querle's gate tower, we might trick our way in. He's extremely stupid.'

'Not that stupid,' objected Two. 'Especially not if Ivar's just got the better of him, he'll be on his mettle.'

'Best to keep looking,' said One. 'I daresay we'll spot a gateway in a week or so. It's always the way; I saw three last week, and today, when I want one, there's nothing to be seen.'

'You didn't see three, I spotted two of them.'

'Oh, hooey. My eyes are much sharper than yours.'

Pebin had been thinking. 'Stop arguing,' he said. 'We haven't got a week or so. Uthar will be up to some trick or other, he's wicked, that guy, full of evil plans. No, we have to push on, and find Ivar as soon as we can.'

'How?'

Scarlet could see from the look on Pebin's face that he was going to come up with something preposterous.

He did.

'We'll borrow a boat,' he said, getting up. 'And we'll sail it through the Causeless Caverns, and into the underground river, the River of Dreams.'

'Creeaaaachh,' went the arpad. 'The River of Dreams? You're mad. And we,' flap, flap, 'are off!'

Eighteen

SCARLET WATCHED THE GREAT TWO-HEADED Sarpad circle up and up and away, over the rooftops.

'The sky's turning a strange colour,' she said. 'Do you think there's going to be a storm?'

She and Pebin looked up into the darkening heavens. Blue was turning into threatening purple, and billowing bronze clouds stretched up into the sky, blocking out the sunlight.

'I don't like the look of it,' said Pebin.

'It's still very hot,' said Scarlet. 'I'm very thirsty, is the water in the fountain okay to drink?'

'Yes,' said Pebin, still staring up at the dramatically changing cloudscape.

'Oh,' said Scarlet. 'The fountain's stopped working.'

'What?' said Pebin. He leant over the edge, looking at the still surface of the water, now dark purple and bronze to reflect the sky. 'This is bad news.'

'I suppose a fountain can just stop working,' said Scarlet. 'A power cut, maybe? There could be an electrical storm.'

'The fountains don't work on power that can be cut,' said Pebin. He looked down the street, and stood up as he saw someone walking towards them. 'Lugh,' he called out. 'My cousin,' he said to Scarlet. 'Just who we need, he's a whizz at soothsaying, he should know if we're likely to find Ivar.'

Lugh was only a little older than Pebin, and shorter, but his face was distant and dreamy, the face of someone much older.

'Soothsayer's face,' whispered Pebin in Scarlet's ear. 'He's in a kind of trance, seeing things that we can't see.'

Lugh looked at them both as though he hurt somewhere very badly. 'You'd better get inside,' he said in a cool and distant voice. 'I can tell you nothing, my foreseeing and far-seeing skills have all gone. The fountains no longer flow, and the Tuan magic is stilled.'

'Why?' said Pebin. 'It's impossible.'

'No, it happened before. When Vemoria's power exceeds its bounds, and the balance is disturbed, then our powers fail. The Gods make it so, for their own purposes.' He shrugged. 'Or out of idle fancy, who can tell?'

'The Tuans are useless without their magic,' said Pebin.

'This is only the beginning,' said Lugh with a great and weary sadness in his voice. 'This time, I doubt if anything can save Tuan and its magic. The old, wild magic is stirring. The Vemorians are calling to it, and if they can find where the last of the Old Kings is imprisoned, and get him into their power, then I think it will be the end for us.'

'I'm not going to be ruled by the Vemorians,' said Pebin, shocked. 'All those rules and regulations, and spies everywhere. It's a terrible way to live.'

'It will be more terrible than that, if the old magic comes back to Vemoria and Tuan and the Gonelands,' said Lugh.

'Who imprisoned the Old King?'

'The Twelve, the original Twelve, when they took control of Vemoria.'

'Then the Vemorians know where he is.'

'No. He was imprisoned by magic, and held by magic. That's Tuan business, not Vemorian. It makes no difference. *We* don't know where he is, so we're helpless.'

He suddenly looked more wide-awake, and asked Pebin where his parents were.

'Dunno,' said Pebin. 'At the college, probably, I expect they're all in a state up there, if what you say is true.'

'Look up,' said Lugh. 'Look into the sky, and see chaos gathering. Get inside, Pebin, you and your schoolfriend.'

'Schoolfriend?' said Scarlet indignantly. 'I'm not a schoolfriend. I'm from Earth.'

'An Otherworlder?' For a moment Lugh's face lit up, and then it became sombre again. 'Watch for an archway, a ford, a mist, and get yourself back into your world and time. It's no place for you here. And if you see my old companions, Hal and Gilly. Or Ben, a redhead like you, then tell them we tried, but the Vemorians and the old ways were too strong.'

'Well, what a doom-and-gloom merchant,' said Scarlet, as Lugh went quickly down a twisting street and out of sight.

'He does tend to know things,' said Pebin, worried. 'I wonder what we ought to do?'

'No question about that,' said Scarlet decisively. 'We'll do exactly what we were planning to do,' said Scarlet. 'Find a boat – at least I don't suppose you were intending to swim down this river of yours, were you? No? Good, because I can't actually swim. I can row, though, so let's get on with it. Before the heavens open and we're soaked.'

Nineteen

*T*HE BOAT WAS A DINGHY. IT WAS CLINKER-built, with a high prow which rose to an elegant point. Like a Viking ship, Scarlet decided, as she hunted around the rocky inlet for the oars. They'll be under a bush, Pebin had said. Ah, there they were.

'You're sure this is your uncle's boat?' She didn't fancy pushing off only to find some furious local running down to the water's edge, calling to them to bring the boat back.

'Nobody will be running anywhere,' said Pebin. 'Didn't you notice all the shutters going up, the shops closing early as we left the city? We aren't the only ones to have seen that sky and to have heard the news that Uthar's on the loose again. The lake and the lakeside will be deserted.'

Scarlet shivered. The air was hot and oppressive and heavy with the threat of terrible storms to come. The lake was utterly still. The water was the colour of blood: purple, de-oxygenated blood.

'Looks like the entrance to the underworld,' she said.

'It more or less is,' said Pebin.

'No other way in to the castle? You're absolutely positive?'

'The river's our only chance, unless we hang around for days. I don't reckon we've got the time.'

Scarlet made a puffing sound, flexed her muscles and

climbed into the boat. 'One oar each, and we'll have to keep looking round to see where we're going. Where *are* we going, by the way?'

'Over there.' Pebin pointed a finger across the lake.

In this light, his eyes seemed almost to glow against the brown of his skin. His curly hair lay damp and dark across his forehead. There was little trace of the lively, light-hearted companion of earlier in the day.

Goodness knew what she looked like, thought Scarlet. She was grateful that she was a long way from any mirror.

Except for the water. When you leaned over the side, a distorted mask of your face looked back at you. Don't lean over, Scarlet told herself, jerking back as she saw her face reflected in a pool of bloody gloom. That was enough to give anyone the heebie-jeebies.

The 'over there' to which Pebin had pointed was a pitch-black patch against the steeply wooded bank on the other side of the lake. Over there looked just like the spot Scarlet would have chosen not to head for.

Pebin released the dinghy, giving it a firm shove with his foot as he let go of the mooring rope. He leapt on board as the boat slid silently into the murky waters. Scarlet, holding his oar as well as hers, waited as he slipped into his place behind her.

The oars dipped into the water with hardly a sound, and they moved out on to the lake.

'No birds,' said Scarlet, concentrating on keeping her stroke in time with Pebin and her movements steady.

'There never are, here,' said Pebin. 'No birds nest on the lakeside, and they never fly over it, either.'

'We aren't likely to see the arpad here, then.'

Pebin grinned. 'No way.'

Crossing to the cave entrance was hard work. It wasn't that far; the lake itself wasn't large. But, as

Scarlet quickly discovered, it was like rowing in treacle. Every stroke was an effort; it felt as though the water was resisting you.

'Ought to send the university boat teams to train here,' she said, breathless. 'They'd think the Thames was a doddle after this.'

'This is terrible,' said Pebin. 'No wonder people don't come here for fun.'

'Why the boat, then?'

'My uncle uses it to cross the lake when he goes into the other part of Tuan. It saves time; the road along here is very hilly.'

'Must be very fit, your uncle.'

Pebin caught a crab, and they were too busy getting themselves back on course for him to answer.

Scarlet turned her head for the umpteenth time to check their route. 'Nearly there,' she said. 'Thank goodness.'

'You may not think that once we get into the caverns,' said Pebin in a gloomy voice.

'Why not?'

'They have a very bad reputation.'

'Have you ever been in them?'

Pebin had to confess that he hadn't.

'Then you'd better wait and see. Your head's been filled full of doomy legends. Bet it's great in there.'

'You really think so?'

'No,' said Scarlet as the boat slid into the icy gloom of the cavern entrance.

Twenty

SURPRISE, SURPRISE.
The cave they were in wasn't black, as Scarlet had expected. 'It's like pewter,' she said. 'Pewter water, pewter walls, pewter stalactites. All grey, with a dull sheen; just like pewter.'

Her voice echoed round the walls. Not in the usual way, with the sound dying away, but with an eerie, metallic sound which grew louder with each repetition. By the time the words came back to her, she and Pebin felt they were being yelled at by some mob equipped with faulty hailers.

PEWTER, TER, TER.

Pebin put a finger on his lips. 'Best not to speak,' he whispered.

An avalanche of deafening S-S-S-S-Ss swept over them. Scarlet blinked, and clapped her hands over her ears.

Big mistake.

Scarlet bent forward desperately to save her oar as it slipped out of the rowlock. Too late; she watched helplessly as it slid into the shiny grey water. A sluggish ripple spread out from where it had vanished.

Dive in and save it, Scarlet thought for one desperate moment.

No way. She knew that if she went into that viscous

liquid she would vanish as completely and swiftly as the oar had done.

'I'll paddle,' mouthed Pebin, stirring his oar like a gondolier to propel the boat through the cavern. His eagerness to be out of that particular cave gave him strength, and the boat shot through the dull-coloured water.

Scarlet felt helpless and useless, now just a passenger in the boat. Pebin seemed to be heading for a low arch of rock to one side, where the water rippled and swirled around a rock. It looked dangerous, but Pebin clearly knew what he was doing, shooting the dinghy past the rock and ducking down as the boat swept out of the pewter cave into some kind of narrow channel.

Scarlet couldn't tell whether the channel was natural or man-made, but as they moved along it, carried by the current of the water flowing in from the cave behind them, the light faded away and they moved into silent darkness.

In what seemed like an hour, but was only in fact a few minutes, Scarlet saw a dim glow, like the light at the end of a railway tunnel. She tried a whisper, and was hugely relieved to find that her voice sounded quite normal.

'Is this the right way?'

'Yes,' said Pebin.

'How do you know?'

'I saw a map, once, at my uncle's house.'

'Where do we go from here?'

'I think there's another underground lake, and the River of Dreams runs out of that.'

'Another cavern?'

'It won't be the same,' said Pebin. 'It never is.'

'Good,' said Scarlet.

'It could be much worse,' said Pebin, as they came to

the end of the channel and the boat shot out into another great cavern.

It was.

That underground lake was most of Scarlet's nightmares come to life. Slimy creatures with far too many legs and glowing, malevolent eyes walked along the rocky shore. Terrifying, black shapes heaved in and out of the water. Dark shadows loomed over her. Locked and barred doors appeared in front of her that she had to open to let the boat through. She could hear sobbing voices, knew she had done some terrible wrong which could never be put right, saw the floating faces of her friends, stained with blood, drifting past the boat.

Scarlet couldn't help herself. She had to get away from these horrors, throw herself into the dark water, end it all.

Pebin's voice came to her from a thousand miles away, urgent, desperate. 'Dream, Scarlet. Good dreams. Wherever's the loveliest place you've ever seen.'

Dark thoughts still flooded into Scarlet's mind. I can't do it, she thought, desperate, distraught. And then she remembered Natar's advice, and let go.

Now into her mind came the image of a photo she had once seen in a travel agent's: an advertisement for some idyllic Indian Ocean retreat. Someone was lying on an air bed in a crystal-clear, turquoise sea; in the distance was a line of sparkling white sand. It was the most beautiful and serene scene, and Scarlet sometimes sent herself to sleep at night by imagining she was on that air bed.

She did so now.

All the terrors vanished instantly, and she relaxed back in the boat, her hand feeling the warm, greeny-blue water. She could feel the sun on her face, hear the call of a sea bird, hear the soft sound of waves lapping on the shore.

'Keep it up,' said Pebin. 'This is wonderful.'

'Let's emigrate,' said Scarlet, never letting up on her vision of a tropical ocean.

'We've done it,' cried Pebin. 'We've crossed it, and now we're under the castle.'

As he spoke, the boat slid through another archway, and sitting up, back in what passed for the real world, Scarlet saw great blocks of stone forming a rough entrance to the river beyond.

'The River of Dreams,' she said. 'Huh, and that was the Lake of Nightmares, I suppose. You could have warned me.'

'I didn't know,' said Pebin. 'Were those your night-mares? I've never had bad dreams like that, they were horrible.'

'You were in my nightmares?'

'Yes. Very strange, I can tell you. I liked the warm blue water, though.'

'Is this river the same?' Scarlet was alarmed; it would take a lot of floating on an air bed to dispel the terrifying images she had passed through on that lake.

'This is a working river,' said Pebin. 'I expect there is some magic about it, but not the same as in the caverns. Those are as old as time. This is a stream which the people in the castle have widened and directed over the centuries. We should be all right.'

'Bit pongy,' said Scarlet, wrinkling up her nose. A nasty thought occurred to her. 'What do these magi-cians in the castle do about sewage, or are they above that kind of thing? I mean, they are human are they? They do eat?'

'There are sewage canals running along the walls,' said Pebin. 'They should be covered up, but they do smell. It's very enclosed here, I think it opens up a bit further along.'

'I blooming well hope so,' said Scarlet indistinctly, since she was holding her nose.

The river was wider now, and the gloom was lightening. 'Where's the light coming from?' Scarlet asked.

'Light shafts, I think,' said Pebin, squinting up into the vault above. 'Yes, you can see them.'

As he spoke, there was a clanking noise. A beam of light fell on to the water, there was a yell of protest, and a dark shape came hurtling down to land in the river with a sickening splash.

Twenty-One

A HEAD BOBBED UP ABOVE THE SURFACE, AND
blew a spout of water out of her mouth. 'Well I
never, not ever, in all my born days.'

Pebin kept the boat as steady as he could while
Scarlet heaved the woman over the side.

'Thank you my dear, I take that very kindly. What a
mercy you were here, otherwise I'd have been swept out
to goodness-knows-where along this nasty river. Whatever are they thinking of, a-tossing of respectable
people down their nasty holes? Oops, there's another of
us.'

There was indeed another beam of light and another
splash. This time the figure who clambered aboard was
a stout man, still in his leather apron and clutching a
bag of tools. He was just as indignant as their first
rescuee.

'What a nerve. I go to the castle, at their request, I
may say, a matter of a faulty door, and when I get
through the gate tower, what happens? They open up
that oubliette affair, and toss me down like I was of no
consequence at all.'

'Oubliette?' said Scarlet.

'Head first into the water, and how do they know I
can swim? They never asked. I won't put up with it,
that's flat. Magicians and sorcerers they may be, but it
doesn't give them the right to go behaving like that.'

'You never spoke a truer word,' the woman said approvingly. 'I know you, you're the carpenter from over on the south side, you did a little job for my cousin Maerie not so long ago.'

'That I did,' said the man, extending a hard-working and still damp hand. 'Well, aren't we lucky that these two youngsters were just coming by in their boat.' He gave Pebin and Scarlet a hard look. 'I do suppose that you aren't magicians? I would be right in that, would I?'

Scarlet and Pebin hastily denied any claims to sorcery or magicianship. Scarlet could feel her thoughtball bulging in her pocket, and hoped that didn't count. She got the feeling that magic of any kind wasn't going to be very popular down here on the river.

'And where might you be heading for?' said the woman. 'I'd take it kindly if you could drop me off *outside* the castle walls, if you're going that way.'

Pebin and Scarlet looked at each other.

'Actually,' said Pebin, 'we came this way to get inside the castle walls. We're looking for a friend, he came into the castle through Querle's gate.'

'Then more fool he,' said the woman. 'A nastier piece of work than that Querle I have yet to meet. If he's one of the castle folk, I'd leave well alone, they've all gone mad up there today. Tossing us out like that. Anything to stop us going inside the inner wall, as if I didn't come and go every day, no trouble to anyone.'

'Why do you come and go?' said Scarlet, holding tight to her seat as the dinghy headed towards the bank with its narrow ledge.

'Difficult to steer,' said Pebin through gritted teeth. 'I don't think we're very well balanced.'

'You're doing a grand job, lad,' said the carpenter. 'I'd give you a hand, only I think if I shifted, we'd all be overboard.'

'Better not,' said Pebin.

'I come and go with paper,' said the woman. 'My family are paper-makers, and those magicians use an awful lot of paper. Best quality, too, they don't stint themselves. Reams and reams I take in. Then I have to bring out the remains, we pulp it down and re-use it, you see.'

Splash!

And another one, right alongside.

'I hope they can swim,' said Pebin. 'The current's quite strong here, and I can't stop.'

Two heads popped up above the water, and in a flail of arms and legs they made for the boat.

'How many will this boat take?' asked Scarlet.

'A few more, yet,' said the carpenter comfortably. 'Well built, she is. My uncle's a boat-builder, I know about boats.'

The new arrivals were a cook and a large dog. There was some argument about heaving the dog on board, but the general sentiment among the oubliette survivors was that if the magicians were against the animal, they should be for it.

'What are they thinking of?' wondered the cook, a thin, spiky woman with a pursed mouth. 'Hurling me down that chute. Whatever's up?'

'General alert, I reckon,' said the paper-maker. 'In a fuss about something, looking for some intruder, that's what I heard. Before they sent me a-whizzing down into the dark waters. Get off!'

This was addressed to the dog, who was standing up on his four large feet, clearly ready for a good shake. He'd send them all flying, thought Scarlet with alarm, but the cook pulled him down to a sitting position and warned him that he'd be overboard if he didn't behave.

'Not that it'd worry him. Born swimming, these gruffhounds.'

'Gruffhound?'

'Yes, he's a gruffhound, all right.'

The animal looked to Scarlet more like a damp woolly rug than anything else, but it had a winning face as well as a vigorous tail and a fine set of teeth.

'That's Wulfstan,' said the carpenter after a careful look.

'Hoebe's dog?'

'It is, too,' chipped in the thin cook. 'That gruffhound came rocketing through the gate, like he always does. Hoebe was way behind; he got turned away, which was lucky for him, in the circumstances, and Wulfstan here was down the chute before he had time to say woof.'

The gruffhound heard that, and gave a deep bark, which reverberated into the vault and then came back to them as though a pack of dogs were hunting through the tunnel.

'Eek,' said the cook. 'This is the strangest place I ever was in, and it doesn't half smell.'

'Drainage,' said the carpenter. 'Not very efficient, the magicians have a mind above that sort of thing.'

'Well, they don't have a mind above panic,' said the paper-maker tartly. 'I never seen such a flap.'

'Vemorians,' said the cook. 'I heard they're worried about Vemorians. They're up to mischief again, tell me something new, and they fancy the Old Kings are coming out of hiding.'

'Get along with you,' said the carpenter. 'There aren't any Old Kings left, and I don't think Vemoria's going to cause any more trouble. They tried it, not so long ago, and much good it did them.'

'It's those Gods meddling again,' said the paper-

—— 83 ——

maker in dark tones. 'If they'd leave us all be, we'd go along fine, and nothing to bother us. Let the magicians carry on with their thises and thats, and we'll get on with what keeps the world ticking along, and we'll all be happy.'

'The Gods don't want us to be happy.'

'It's not a matter of wanting or not wanting,' said the carpenter wisely. 'It's indifference. They just don't care. They never have and they never will, and that's an end to it.'

'And an end to us, too,' shrieked the cook, as the by now familiar light flashed out directly above them, and another tumbling body came straight down towards the boat.

Twenty-Two

*T*HEY CRINGED, WAITING FOR THE CRASH, THE water to come pouring in, the capsized dinghy to be swept away by the the currents.

Scarlet, hanging tightly on to the gruffhound, was the first to notice that the hefty shape heading for them was heading no more. In its place was a large, brightly coloured feather, which floated gently down to land on the bench beside the paper-maker.

'Dang it, a witch,' she said, as the feather grew in width and height, and transformed itself back into a person.

'It's Mab,' said the cook. 'What are you doing in these parts, Mab? I thought you never came out of the south, not since that time with that head, that was a wicked business.'

The new arrival didn't look in the least bit like a witch to Scarlet. But then she had to admit that she'd never seen a witch. Not to know it, in any case. Mab looked exactly like one of her teachers at school. Ordinary. Not likely to stand out in a crowd. How could she be a witch?

'Hello, young Pebin,' said Mab. 'How's your mum and dad keeping? And young Lugh?'

'Um, hello, Mab,' said Pebin. 'I didn't know you were in the Walled City. Nobody said.'

'Well, I wasn't,' said Mab cheerfully. 'Not until I got

a message this morning from the castle. Come at once, we need to ask some questions. Now, I learned a good long while ago that when magicians summon you, it's best to go, straight away. Because if you don't, it can get a bit tricky.'

'You're right there,' said the paper-woman.

'Woof,' said the gruffhound.

'Quiet,' said the cook.

'Being invited, I didn't expect there to be any trouble, so I got a shock when they opened up that hole they've got in all the courtyards and just tossed me down. No explanations, no ceremony, no apologies; just whoosh and clang with the lid, and that's me heading down towards this boat to the general dismay of all concerned. Don't deny it, *I* saw your faces.'

'We thought you were going to land smack in the boat,' protested Pebin. '*You*'d have been alarmed if you were us.'

'Maybe, maybe,' said Mab. 'Although it takes a lot to alarm a witch.' She produced a bag of sweets from one of the many large pockets on the sleeveless top she was wearing. 'Humbug, anyone?'

Twenty-Three

*W*HILE OTHERS WERE LEAVING THE CASTLE faster and more uncomfortably than they would have chosen, Ivar was winding his way through it. He wasn't lost; demigods don't get lost, but he was mystified. Demigods, as Immortals, took no notice of anyone or anything except the Gods. Who by and large left them alone, having their own feuds and plans to occupy their time.

In theory.

In practice, there wasn't a single Immortal that Ivar knew or knew of who wouldn't think twice before venturing into the castle.

The castle was legendary. Those from the Third Lands and the Land of the Gods didn't have much to do with magic as practised on the other side of the Spellbound Gorge. Mere mortals' nonsense, they would claim. And yet Ivar felt uneasy. He knew that the magic which had built and bound the castle was partly the old magic, and even the demigods weren't keen on chaos.

When the old and wild magic was stirred together with the sophisticated arts of the Tuans, then you had a powerful mix.

Ivar wished he had his bones. He'd feel better with his bones inside him, well, anyone would. If he had his bones, of course, he wouldn't be here. Which would be best for all concerned.

Trust malicious Ril to bring his skeleton here, and Ivar was sure that was what he'd done. He knew that it would take a lot to entice Ivar out of his natural territory and into the castle. Trust Ril to make friends with a creep like Querle.

Ivar slunk through another tiny yard, like the bottom of a well, he thought sourly, looking at the walls which towered above him. Still, at least he could see the sky, which was an improvement. He must be out of reach of all those watchmen and guards and gatekeepers who'd been skipping round in circles trying to stop him coming in.

Idiots. And why were they in such a frenzy about him? All right, they didn't like an Immortal wandering about the place, but it wasn't just that. It was all Querle's fault. He'd sounded the alarm. And why had he done that? Because he knew that Ivar was in the right place to find his bones. Ril didn't want Ivar to find his bones. Ril would take it out on Querle if Ivar's hunt was successful.

Serve him right.

Time for a slump, he thought. Time to rest his aching muscles, really, the thoughtlessness of Ril. All right, maybe losing your head and having it carried round in a basket for a few days was uncomfortable, but it couldn't have been as bad as this.

Oh, no, what was that looking down at him?

What had four golden eyes, two sharp beaks, a large body and the usual number of claws for an eagle?

Good lord, the arpad. Ivar lolled to one side as the great creature landed beside him and hopped across the stone slabs to steady itself.

'Greetings,' said Beak One.

'O demigod,' added Two, who liked to be courteous.

'What is an arpad doing in the castle?' said Ivar. 'Out of bounds for you lot, isn't it?'

'Strictly speaking, yes,' said Beak One.

'Maybe,' said Beak Two. 'But these are troubled times.'

Ivar thought about that. 'They didn't seem especially troubled when I came through the gate a bit earlier on. Except about me being here. What's up?'

'Uthar of Vemoria is on the move.'

'Oh, him. What a tiresome fellow he is. Is that dreadful daughter of his still with him?'

'She is.'

'Well, these petty squabbles between Vemoria and Tuan are nothing to do with me. You haven't noticed my bones by any chance, have you? As you've flown about? Seen any skeletons which look as though they could do with a body?'

'Most skeletons look that way,' said Two with a loud screech of laughter which was immediately echoed by One.

'No petty squabble,' said Beak Two, shaking his head. 'Uthar plans to unleash the power of the Old Kings.'

'Provided he can find the only one left.'

'Ah,' said Ivar. 'Him.'

'You know him, don't you?'

'I haven't seen him for a very long time. He's half an Otherworlder, isn't he?'

'So they say.' The arpad gave a quick flutter of its wings. 'You know where he is, don't you?'

'I'm not interested in Old Kings,' said Ivar with a flash of irritation. 'What I'm interested in is my bones. And I'm sure they're around here somewhere. I've got a tingling feeling, I just know they're about.'

'Pins and needles,' said Beak One helpfully.

'Try rubbing the afflicted part,' said Two.

'Oh, go away,' said Ivar, flapping a droopy arm at the arpad.

'If someone helped you to find your bones, would you help them to find the Old King?'

Ivar shot the arpad a suspicious look. 'I might.'

'That's all right, then,' said One. 'Now, what you need is a nose.'

'He's got a nose,' said Two, after a moment's inspection.

'Not his own nose. A trained nose. The nose of one bred to smell out bones.'

'My bones don't smell.'

'They will have a bony scent,' said One tactfully. 'Enough for the right nose to sniff them out.'

'And where is this specially wonderful nose?'

'An intelligent hound is what you want.'

Ivar thought for a moment. 'Not such a bad idea,' he said grudgingly. 'Only where do I find a hound?'

'That's a good question. And one that I can answer.'

'Do so, then.'

'It just so happens that there's a gruffhound running loose about the place.'

'A gruffhound, eh? You may just be on to something here, arpad. Gruffhounds have a very keen sense of smell.'

'Intelligent, too.'

'Not very intelligent if it's running in circles about the castle.'

'Not in circles, no. It was looking for its master, Hoebe.'

'And?'

'And Hoebe never made it through the castle gate. The gruffhound did, he didn't.'

'And?'

'And they tossed the gruffhound down an oubliette.'

Ivar fell back into a heap. 'What use to me is a dead gruffhound?'

'That's the point, he'll have landed in the river.'

'What river?'

'The underground river. The River of Dreams. And he won't drown. Gruffhounds swim. They swim very well.'

'So?'

'So, let's go down to the river and find him.'

Twenty-Four

*T*HE BOAT WENT ON ITS HAPHAZARD WAY ALONG the river. Pebin had very little control of it now; the eddies and currents were too varied and strong for him to cope with.

Mab wasn't at all bothered. 'Let it go, Pebin. We'll hit the bank eventually, and then we can get off.'

'Get off?' The carpenter wasn't too happy about that.

Nor was the cook. 'Not this side of the walls, I don't.'

'Best to stay on until we come out at Wastelake, that's out of reach of this castle lot.' The paper-maker was firm.

'We *want* to be in the castle,' protested Scarlet. 'That's why we're here.'

The cook, the carpenter and the paper-maker looked at her in astonishment. The cook tapped her forehead with a knowing finger.

'Mad,' she said.

'Crazy.'

'Needs counselling.'

'I don't,' said Scarlet. 'And we're not mad. We're looking for someone who's in the castle.'

'Stop fretting,' said Mab. 'I reckon we're going to bump into that landing stage just along there. You and Pebin and I can go ashore, and the boat can go on.'

'What about the dog?'

'That's Hoebe's dog.'

'Leave him with us, we'll see he gets home.'

'Nasty great thing.'

'We'll take him,' said Pebin. 'He could be useful. Mab, why do you want to get off?'

'Well, you know how it is, dear, running water and I don't mix. I'm not supposed to cross it, and even floating along like this is doing nothing for my well-being. Besides, you might need my help.'

'Help! You witches don't help anyone,' said the paper-maker accusingly. 'It's you and those magicians and all the rest of them that cause the trouble. We'd be all right if it weren't for you and your subtle tricks.'

'We're to blame for everything, are we?' said Mab. 'Gone-off food, unruly teenagers and the common cold, I suppose. Just what kind of a witch do you think I am?'

In a flash, she was gone, and in her place was an old hag with rheumy eyes, clawed hands and a single, fanged tooth, bent double in a black cloak.

'Urgh,' said the paper-maker.

'Where is she?' said Scarlet. 'What's happened?'

'Mab, stop it!' said Pebin.

'Or a nice toad,' said Mab, transforming herself in a flash into the largest and most hideous-looking creature possible.

Scarlet liked toads, but she didn't like this one at all.

'Or there's the sultry type,' said Mab, becoming a gold-haired enchantress with a sexy smoulder.

This was all too much for the other passengers. As the boat bumped gently into the landing stage, just as Mab had said it would, they clambered off the boat and stood in a cross threesome, glaring at Mab.

'You silly lot,' she said, transforming herself back into her normal self. 'We're the ones who are getting off, not you.'

'She's right.'

'I'm not staying in that boat with her.'

'You get off, and we'll get back in.'

Just like musical chairs, thought Scarlet, as they edged round each other in their efforts to swap places. The gruffhound had sat solidly through the proceedings, but at a word from Mab he joined them on the wooden landing stage.

'Bye,' said Mab, waving cheerfully as the boat was drawn out into the current again. 'If things go badly, I expect we'll meet up as slaves in the quarries of Vemoria.'

That brought wails of fear and dismay from the boat, but in no time it had shot round the next bend and was out of sight.

'What a useless bunch,' said Mab, brushing some of the wetness off her long red skirt.

What a place, thought Scarlet. They were still standing on the slippery wooden landing stage. Behind them was an arched doorway, and behind that steps led up to goodness knew where. A dully flaming torch glimmered in a sconce on the heavy stone wall. Everything was clammy and wet, and water splashed down from the dim vaults overhead to make eerie plopping noises on the damp wooden planking.

Mab wasn't at all bothered by their surroundings. 'Fill me in, Pebin. Who exactly are we looking for? Why? Where is he?'

Scarlet dug her feet in. 'Hold on, I've got a few questions to ask.'

'Be quick about it,' said Mab. 'We've got work to do.'

'Who are you, for a start?'

'This is Mab, my aunt,' said Pebin, not looking too happy about it.

'Everyone has funny relations,' said Scarlet.

'I am not a funny relation,' said Mab.

'No, no, she didn't mean it like that,' said Pebin hastily. 'Don't go off again, Mab, please. No more shape-changing, *please*.'

'I don't think I could, to be honest,' said Mab. 'Things are very odd once you're standing on castle ground.'

Mab looked perfectly normal. Scarlet couldn't be sure of her age, she didn't seem either young or old. She wasn't tall or short, her hair was brown, and her slightly chubby cheeks were rosy red. She looked a comfortable sort of person, the kind you wouldn't give a second look to in the High Street.

Except that motherly types in the High Street didn't have piercing eyes, nor could they be feathers one minute and warty toads the next.

'We witches aren't very high on the scale of power,' said Mab. 'And I'm not a topnotch witch, not one of the high fliers. Although my spells mostly work, and I can do several excellent deceits. Still, I'm all you've got, and I must be necessary to whatever it is you're up to, or I wouldn't be here.'

'That's true,' said Pebin, brightening a little. He turned to Scarlet. 'Don't look so doubtful, Scarlet. Mab'll be a help, I bet you.'

'Oh, well,' said Scarlet, unconvinced, but knowing there wasn't much she could do about it.

'We're looking for a demigod called Ivar,' explained Pebin.

'Him!' said Mab in tones of scorn. 'He's a useless fellow if ever there was one. What's he been up to, and why is he in the castle? Mostly that lot won't come near here, far too lazy, apart from anything else.'

'He's lost his bones. Some other demigod nicked them, for revenge I think.'

'Ha, and I know who that will be,' said Mab. 'Tsk, tsk. Where are these bones?'

'He must think they're here. He was hunting for them, and he came through a gate tower.'

'That's who the castle officials were looking for. That's why they were tossing us all down the oubliettes. It's too bad, it really is. Why are you interested in Ivar and his bones? It's not your problem.'

'We're looking for a red-haired man. Natar said we had to find him, so that Scarlet here can go back to her world.'

'Aha,' said Mab, her eyes narrowing as she looked at Scarlet. 'Another Red One, is it?'

'I don't know what you mean,' said Scarlet uncomfortably.

'It'll be the prisoner you're looking for,' said Mab, suddenly brisk.

'Ivar knows where he is,' said Scarlet. 'So Natar said.'

'Only Ivar, having a brain that can only hold one thought at a time, isn't going to tell you anything about any prisoner until he's got his skeleton back. Right?'

'That's it.'

'So now we need to find him,' said Scarlet.

'Tricky,' said Mab. 'The castle's a big place, and a complete maze. It could take days to go round it, and you still mightn't find him.'

'Scarlet's got a thoughtball,' said Pebin with some pride.

Mab gave Scarlet a sharp look. 'You have, have you? And what use is that to an Otherworlder? And where did you get it?'

'From Natar,' said Scarlet.

'And she can use it,' said Pebin. 'She needs to practise, but she can use it, I've seen her.'

'Very peculiar,' said Mab. 'Are you sure you're an Otherworlder?'

'I don't belong here, I can tell you that,' said Scarlet. What a nerve, this witchy woman questioning her like this.

Mab held up a silencing finger. 'Listen,' she said. 'I hear a shuffling sound.'

'Grrrff,' said the gruffhound, who was lying patiently at their feet.

'What is it?' said Pebin.

'Sounds like someone with no feet and a heavy bag.'

'It sounds like Ivar,' said Mab.

'It is,' said Pebin, as the three of them gazed up the steep flight of worn stone steps, to see Ivar's bendy figure at the top of them.

Twenty-Five

*I*VAR LOLLED AGAINST THE WALL AS THE THREE OF them came up the steps. Wulfstan had taken the flight in three leaps and was waiting at the top for them to join him.

'An untidy dog,' said Ivar.

Wulfstan bared his teeth.

'If you want his help, you'd better be civil,' said Mab.

'To a hound?'

'To anyone who can help you, Ivar the Boneless. In your situation and condition you can't go about offending anyone or anything. Now, we find your bones, you take us to the prisoner, that's the deal.'

Ivar wasn't listening, or so it seemed. He didn't want to be pinned down, he'd think about it when he had his bones, and besides, he wasn't exactly sure he'd be able to find the prisoner. 'Tricky, the Old Kings.'

'No bargain, no bones.'

'Immortals don't bargain,' said Ivar, suddenly haughty. 'Ever. It's unheard of.'

'I never heard of an Immortal without any bones. There's a first time for everything.' Mab was firm.

'Oh, very well,' said Ivar, ruffling the back of the gruffhound's neck with a saggy hand.

Wulfstan growled.

'See?' said Ivar. 'Pointless. Well, doggie, how are you on bones?'

'Doggie?' said Mab. 'None of that. I wouldn't call you bendy-man.'

I would, thought Scarlet, and she could see from Pebin's face that he would, too. Ivar had seemed better company when they were out in the city, in the sunshine. Getting het up about his blinking bones, no doubt; well, you couldn't blame him for that.

Pebin crouched down in front of the hound and took his head in his hands so that he could look into his liquid brown eyes. 'Bones,' he said very slowly and clearly. 'Do you understand the word bones?'

Wulfstan's tail thumped against the ground, and he gave a pleased pant.

'Poof,' said Pebin, recoiling. 'I don't like to think what you had for breakfast. Here,' he went on, heaving Wulfstan across to Ivar. 'Put out your hand,' he said. 'So that the gruffhound can smell it.'

Wulfstan obviously didn't think that Ivar would make a good breakfast; he wrinkled his dark, wet nose and sneezed, loudly and messily.

'Disgusting animal,' said Ivar, pulling out a yellow silk handkerchief and flicking his arm with it.

Pebin took no notice. 'Ivar. Bones. Good Wulfstan. Find Ivar's bones.'

Wulfstan rose from his haunches, stretched his long, shaggy legs out in front of him and yawned widely, finishing up with a squealing noise as he snapped his jaws shut. Then he shook his head, gave himself a good scratch with a back leg, sniffed around the stonework, and set off at a cracking pace.

'Move,' said Pebin. 'We mustn't lose sight of him.'

Never had a castle been so full of bones.

The gruffhound's first port of call was the kitchens. A few scared-looking minions were bustling round with trays and staggering under the weight of great serving dishes, but they made themselves scarce when Wulfstan came through the door.

He was followed by a surprisingly fleet Ivar, looking more contorted than ever, Mab, quite worn out by moving at such speed, and Pebin and Scarlet bringing up the rear.

It was a sensible place to head for, in Scarlet's opinion, if you were bone-hunting, but Ivar and Mab weren't impressed, though they checked the larders and the great stock pot simmering on the fire, just to make sure. 'If they've cooked my bones . . .' said Ivar threateningly.

There were bones in plenty. Dinosaur bones, some of them, Scarlet reckoned. Could anything have a leg bone that big? Tiny bones. Even a china bone, although none of them could work out what it was doing there.

'Come on, Wulfstan,' said Pebin, dragging the hound away from a particularly tasty-looking bone which he had unearthed from one of the larders. 'No time for that now. Ivar's bones, Wulfstan. *Ivar's*.'

The gruffhound was hauled reluctantly away from the kitchen, and after a few tacks to and fro, and much sniffing of the air, he set off once more at a good old pace.

'Seems to know where he's going,' said Scarlet, jogging alongside Pebin. Ivar, moving with the strange, rolling step of a long distance walk-racer, was well ahead of them, while Mab, grumbling discontentedly, had fallen way behind.

Wulfstan gave an excited yelp, and put on a spurt, vanishing round a corner with a scrape and clatter of his claws on the smooth stone. He came to an abrupt halt beside a huge wooden door, covered in studs. Then he stood on his back legs and scrabbled violently at the door with his big front paws.

'Ha,' said Ivar. 'Maybe this dunderhead of a dog is on to something.'

'It's a very big door,' said Pebin, looking at it with awe.

Scarlet gave it an experimental shove with her shoulder, but it moved not a fraction.

'Locked,' said Ivar.

Scarlet took the great brass ring at the centre with both hands, and turned it while Pebin pushed.

It didn't shift.

'I told you, it'll be locked,' said Ivar with some satisfaction. 'They'd be sure to lock my bones away, Ril wouldn't just leave them lying around.'

A thin, frightened-looking man in a drab brown tunic scuttled along the passage towards them, cast them an alarmed look and increased his speed.

Ivar put out a hand to stop him, but he swerved round him. 'Can't stop, general emergency, got to get on,' he said in a wispy, croaky voice.

Pebin was more effective; he put out a foot, and caused the man to stumble.

'Must get on,' he whimpered.

'Answer a question first. We're looking for a skeleton. Is it here?'

The man cast a scared look up and down the corridor. 'Through that door,' he whispered. 'That's where your skeleton will be. Must get on, the Vemorians are coming, we'll all be skeletons soon enough, alack, alack.'

'What a depressing fellow,' said Ivar. 'I hope he's right, and that my skeleton's on the other side of this door.'

Mab arrived at a dignified speed. 'What's this? What's up?'

'The gruffhound led us here,' said Scarlet, patting Wulfstan's head.

'Open the door, then.'

'We can't. I've pushed, and we've tried the handle and Pebin's pushed. It won't budge.'

'Locked,' said Ivar.

'Nonsense,' said Mab, going up to the door and seizing the brass ring handle. 'Pushed have you? How about pulling?' She bent her knees and gave the door a good yank, and with a groaning, grinding sound, it moved towards her.

'Ah,' said Pebin. 'I see. Pull, then.'

He and Scarlet laid hold of the ring and pulled with all their might. The door swung effortlessly open, sending them staggering back to land in a heap on top of Ivar.

'Get off,' he said furiously. 'As if it wasn't enough not to have bones, I have to have two hooligans landing on top of me. Where are my bones?'

This last cry of anguish was answered by Mab, who pursed up her mouth and made a whistling sound. 'Um,' she said, peering through the door.

'Well?' said Ivar, wavering to his feet and heading for the gap.

'Ah,' said Mab. 'Maybe not quite what we're looking for.'

The door opened on to one of the many enclosed courtyards which were scattered about the castle. It was lighter than the dim passages, although not much, since massed and sultry clouds were gathered in the sky above. There was grass underfoot, and stones.

'Is that a well?' said Scarlet, looking at the little domed structure in the centre.

'No,' said Pebin, laughing. 'That gruffhound's really led us astray this time.'

'Why?' said Scarlet.

'Can't you see?' said Pebin.

Ivar was dancing a rubbery dance of pain and fury. 'Idiotic dog. Of all the stupid creatures, just let me get my hands on him . . .'

Mab was laughing too. 'He's a very intelligent hound, very clever indeed. We've asked him to find bones; in fact, a skeleton, and he's led us to the very place. Lots of skeletons here.'

'Where?' Scarlet was beginning to have a suspicion of where they were, although it wasn't exactly like the ones back in her world. However, there was a look to the place which was familiar.

'It's a graveyard,' said Pebin, beside himself with laughter. 'Well done, Gruffo, you've brought us to the dead centre of the castle.'

'Oh, very funny,' said Ivar.

Twenty-Six

*I*N FARAWAY VEMORIA, UTHAR PACED.
He was in the great council chamber, and one of his shoes squeaked slightly against the black, polished marble floor. Behind the table which stretched across one end of the hall sat Culun, Uthar's Chancellor and right-hand man.

Culun watched his master, noting every step. He didn't feel threatened by Uthar's dark and brooding appearance; he was all too used to it. He noticed, though, that new harsh lines had become etched in his face, joining the others accumulated over half a lifetime of power and aggression and plotting.

Uthar slammed a fist into his other hand. 'We have to find Merleon.'

Outside, two men stood guard by the massive black metal doors of the council chamber. Doors to keep an army out, but doors that were not completely closed.

'Who's this Merleon?' whispered one of the guards, a young man doing his first term of duty at the council chamber.

The second guard was an old hand. 'That's not a name you mention out loud. He's the last of the Old Kings, the ones that got overthrown when the first Twelve took over in Vemoria. They banished all the sorcerers, and the Old Kings vanished for ever. This one is half Otherworlder, and he was imprisoned, held by magic, over the border.'

'Why do they want to find him, then?'

The old guard shrugged. 'Who knows? It'll be for some mischief, that's for sure. Now be quiet, I want to listen.'

Uthar was shouting at Culun. 'Why haven't the spies sent back word?'

'They have no word to send.'

'Terminate them. Send others.'

'There are no others. These are the only ones left. And they are the best; what they can't discover, no one can.'

'No one!' Uthar turned on his heel and banged a hand down on the table in front of Culun, who remained unmoved. He knew better than to show the least flicker of alarm. One chink, and he'd be thrown into the dungeons with all the others. If he was lucky, and a grimmer fate didn't await him.

Uthar was grinding on. 'All the rest of the Twelve exiled, destroyed, discredited. I have Vemoria in my hands. A new era beckons, a time of ultra-control, ultra-prosperity, ultra-expansion. An end to Tuan, the Gonelands turned into a colony of slaves; all this I can do, but I must have Merleon. With Merleon I have the old magic, and with that I have complete control.'

'Ultra, ultra control,' said the guard outside the door, under his breath.

'Our army is strong.'

'Our army cannot fight against sorcerers and magicians and all that scum. I need the old magic to let loose on them, to sweep them away. And that means I need Merleon.'

'Merleon may not agree. Merleon survived alone among the Old Kings because he was a rebel.'

'Merleon is a captive. If he becomes *my* prisoner then he's in my power. He will find it worth his while to do the one or two simple things I ask of him. I must have the Dewstone, and only one of that red-headed brood can reclaim the Dewstone. I must be able to bring back the old city. The Galat of the Old Kings, with its towers and magic webs of influence. How otherwise can I rule as I want?'

Good question, thought Culun. He said nothing, and the shrewd little eyes almost lost in the folds of his chubby cheeks gave nothing away.

'Where is Erica?'

'Gone to gather news.'

'I didn't order her to do that.'

'Erica is your daughter, Uthar. She follows her own orders.'

'It can do no harm.'

Don't you be too sure, thought Culun. Foul Erica, always snooping and noticing. Always fomenting trouble with her sharp tongue and ungenerous spirit. What a terrible pair he had to serve. Still, he was up and about, with a substantial meal tucked away beneath his belt, which was more than you could say for most of his former colleagues.

'We leave tonight,' said Uthar finally, after a few more turns about the hall. 'That girl is in the Walled City, I have had news of that, at least. From Requin; good to know that *someone* keeps me informed. If I have her, then I have Merleon in my grasp.'

'Can you be so sure?'

A look from Uthar was enough. Culun rose from the table. 'Very well,' he said, bowing as he gathered his papers together.

'Summon a force of the Guard. We must travel fast.'

'Travel? Where to?'

'To the Walled City, idiot. That's where we will find news of Merleon. We know that the chains of magic which bind Merleon were forged by that foul bunch of sorcerers in the Walled City.'

'With so much power in his hands, it's a strange choice to remain a prisoner.'

'Ha!' said Uthar. 'The fool. He can escape from captivity at any time by using the old, wild magic. Only he won't do it.' He banged a fist into the palm of his other hand. 'He won't do it, because to do so would be to unleash wild forces across Tuan and Vemoria and the Gonelands, and he won't do that.'

'A man of principle.' Culun was surprised.

'Scruples,' spat Uthar. 'So stupid. So unnecessary. But if we have the girl, then I think he will listen to reason.'

'If the magicians know where he's imprisoned, will they tell you? How can you persuade them to reveal this information?'

'Everyone has their price,' said Uthar with certainty. 'Everyone is corruptible, even magicians. Once they see where their interests lie. Once they realize the strength of our forces, and realize that not all their spells can prevent their precious city being razed to the ground, then they'll find they're feeling helpful.'

I wouldn't be too sure, thought Culun, as he padded out of the hall after his master. He noticed that the doors had not been fully closed. He looked at the two guards, committing their rigid faces to memory.

Such men might be useful.

Culun liked to hedge his bets.

Twenty-Seven

*T*HEY RETRACED THEIR STEPS BACK TO THE kitchens. Ivar objected, but Pebin insisted.

'I'm starving. Hunting for bones is hungry work, and the graveyard was a shock to the system.'

'Traumatic,' agreed Scarlet. She didn't think Mab was against the idea, either; Mab looked the sort who would feel peckish at regular intervals.

'As long as there's something I recognize.' Scarlet hadn't altogether liked the look of some of the food she had seen.

'That's because you were poking round in the magicians' larder. Some of these types here are into seaweed and weird plants.'

'To eat, or for spells?'

'Who knows?' said Mab. 'Strange are the ways of magicians.'

'And not of witches?'

'We witches,' said Mab, 'are completely normal as far as our eating habits go. And we don't use seaweed or anything else for spells, our spells are woven in the mind.'

'What mind?' said Pebin under his breath, which earned him a sharp look from his aunt. 'Sorry,' he said, grinning at her. 'I don't mean it.'

'Better not,' said Mab, leading the way into the kitchen.

It was still deserted. News of the Vemorian threat – 'which, frankly, my dears, I don't believe in,' said Mab – had presumably sent the staff into hiding or out of the castle and home to comparative safety.

Much to Scarlet's relief, there was plenty of food of a recognizable sort. Freshly baked loaves of bread, jars of honey and jam, cheese which seemed all right even to Scarlet's suspicious tastes, apples and plums and some little yellow fruits which she had never seen and certainly never eaten.

'Is it all right to eat the fruit?' said Pebin.

'Why not?' Mab bit into a tiny tart, filled with cream and little purple berries and covered with a powdering of sugar.

'They say that if you eat magic apples, you get into all kinds of trouble.'

'In the Third Lands, yes; I never heard of it happening here.'

'Um,' said Pebin, but Scarlet noticed that he none-theless gave the apples a miss.

Scarlet had no such inhibitions. As they loaded their pockets with supplies for later, she added several apples to her collection.

'Now where?' said Ivar, who had picked at this and that with a fastidious reluctance until Mab pointed out that he needed to keep his strength up.

'Very strenuous, moving about minus a skeleton.'

'I'm glad someone appreciates the situation,' said Ivar. 'It's agony, sheer agony, and such an effort. I'll never forgive Ril, never.'

'Think how wonderful you'll feel when you get your bones back.'

'If, not when. I have to say, I'm feeling decidedly pessimistic about this. Hours of searching, and not a sign of my skeleton, it's too bad.'

'It's probably in a very obvious place,' said Scarlet. 'You always miss things in the obvious place.'

'And where, pray, is the obvious place for a skeleton to be?' asked Ivar crossly.

Scarlet laughed. 'Oh, it has to be a skeleton in the cupboard, doesn't it?'

'Very funny. I do applaud your and Pebin's sense of humour, most entertaining, I'm sure.'

The gruffhound, who had also stocked up while in the kitchen, was set to work with further instructions about Ivar and bones.

'I don't think he has a clue what he's supposed to be searching for,' grumbled Ivar.

Scarlet flared up in Wulfstan's defence. 'He's a very intelligent dog, anyone can see that. Aren't you, Wulfstan?'

She got a slobbery lick from the hound for that, before he went back to his nose-down-tail-swishing, tacking-to-and-fro mode. Then he lifted his head, gave a short bark and set off along a narrow passage, which twisted and turned in a most confusing manner.

'Are we going up?' Scarlet said to Pebin.

'Feels like it, and it's getting quite slippery.'

Mab wasn't too happy about that. 'It could be difficult if we meet anyone coming the other way.'

They didn't. The path ran on its strange way which ended in a low arch and a tiny, round, stone room. They didn't all fit into it, and Mab and Scarlet peered in, trying to see if there was any way out except the way they had come.

'No,' said Mab.

'There must be,' said Pebin. 'Look at the way Wulfstan is sniffing.'

'Try running your hands round the wall,' suggested Mab.

Ivar was good at that, patting the chilly stone curved wall with his floppy hands. He went slowly round, collecting dust and cobwebs, but nothing else. Then, when he was an armstretch from where he'd started, there was a click, and a section of the wall rolled back into the curve.

'Steps,' said Scarlet. Presumably they'd have to see where they led, and it seemed a likely hidey-hole, but just the same, she didn't like the look of them.

'They go up for miles,' said Pebin, peering upwards.

Mab sighed. 'This is more exercise than I take in a week. And I have a suspicion I know what's up at the top. Still it's worth a try.'

'Something wicked up there, do you think?' said Scarlet, following closely on Mab's heels.

'Someone, more like,' said Mab. 'And not wicked so much as full of plots and devious ideas.'

'Oh,' said Scarlet.

Ivar didn't hesitate when he reached the top step and saw a double door. He gave a loud cry of 'Bones!' and gave the door as much of a shove as a boneless man could.

The doors opened with eerie silence, and Ivar disappeared through them, with the gruffhound bounding after him.

Twenty-Eight

'A H,' SAID PEBIN. 'BEST TO WAIT HERE AND SEE
what happens.'

'Coward,' said Scarlet, trying to see into the room.

'Not so,' said Pebin. 'Just cagey; Ivar may need our
help if it's a trap. We can be of use out here, but not in
there with him.'

Scarlet squeezed past him. Another cry of 'Bones!'
from within was encouraging, and, taking a deep
breath, she crossed the threshold.

Anybody would have known the room for a magician's lair. It was exactly like every magician's room in
every spooky film or comic book.

The octagonal tower room with black walls festooned
with stars and glowing pentacle. The round skylight
with dark blue glass breaking up the light into grotesque
patterns on the floor below. A big table, piled high with
strange objects, papers, dishes of unidentifiable sub-
stances. And a huge black cat snoozing on a black
velvet cushion. Scarlet wouldn't have known it was
there if it hadn't opened its tawny eyes, given them a
golden blink and blended back into the blackness again.

'Wow,' said Scarlet.

There was a fire lit in a wide, black fireplace. No
ordinary fire, this, Scarlet noted, as she watched the
flickering green and blue and copper-coloured flames.

There was a man sitting in a high-backed wooden

chair beside the fire, and he didn't look in the least as Scarlet would have expected the occupant of such a room to look.

No lean, bony face, no dark hooded eyes, no long fingers and ugly nose.

He was a neat man, good-looking in a wiry way, thought Scarlet, dressed in a wine-coloured velvet coat. His eyes were dark, his hair grey and black and wavy; not long, not short.

His voice, now, that was different. 'Like velvet,' Pebin said afterwards, when they compared notes.

'Come in,' the man said, with an elegant wave of his hand towards a fretful Ivar. 'I hope you've come to take your wavy friend away.'

Pebin had followed Scarlet into the room. 'Ivar thinks his bones are in here.'

'I'm afraid not,' said the man with a faint smile. 'Bones, hardly. Very uncivilized to keep bones about the place, I feel.'

Ivar, who'd been hunting about the room in one direction while Wulfstan made a circuit in the other, came to a halt in front of the man. 'I', he said in ringing tones, 'am a demigod.'

The man sighed. 'One can always tell,' he said.

'And these aren't any old bones I'm looking for; they're my bones. My skeleton.'

'Careless, to lose one's skeleton,' observed the man.

'It was taken,' said Ivar, sulky now.

'Well, I assure you, I haven't taken your bones.'

'I know you haven't. Ril took them. He's hidden them in the castle, I know he has, and where better than in here?'

'I can think of a thousand places better than in here, now you come to mention it,' said the man.

So polite, thought Scarlet, and those dark eyes so

vicious and penetrating. And what had happened to Mab?

The man saw her eyes flick to the entrance. 'Another in your party? Do ask her or him to join us.'

Pebin looked out of the door. 'She isn't there. Mab!' he called.

'My dear friend Mab, not really? How strange of her to keep away.'

'I expect she's lost,' said Pebin.

'Your aunt, isn't she? Oh, yes, you're Pebin. I know you, young man. We hear about the young hopefuls studying for greater things. Not doing very well, are you? Well, life as a farmer is hard, but you'll get enough to eat. Unless your farming is as bad as your soothsaying, in which case you'll go hungry.'

'Why are you so rude?' said Scarlet furiously.

The man looked at her as though he was seeing her properly for the first time. For a brief second, as his eyes rested on her flaming hair, he looked startled; now why? Scarlet asked herself. She didn't like the aura of menace surrounding him, she didn't like the indifferent cruelty lurking in his dark eyes, she didn't like the way he had lashed out at Pebin.

'A redhead,' the man said. 'Very interesting.' The tone of his voice was an insult. 'I suggest you all remove yourselves. There are no bones here, Ivar, and if I have anything to do with it you'll never find your skeleton. A half-useless demigod is much better than the usual kind.'

There was a loud yowl and much hissing. The gruffhound had wandered too near to the huge black cat. Now he was rolling in a shaggy heap, trying to shake the cat off his back.

Scarlet leapt to the hound's rescue, scolding and shouting at the cat and pulling Wulfstan away.

'I think we'd better go,' said Pebin, shaken.

'Good idea,' said Scarlet, casting a last, baleful glance at the man as she licked the blood from the scratched hand.

The doors shut behind them as though closed by an unseen hand.

'What a scary place,' said Pebin.

'Grim man.'

'Rude and unhelpful,' said Ivar.

'Woof,' said Wulfstan, taking a quick lick at a sore spot where the cat had neatly removed a patch of his fur.

They clattered back down the steps to find Mab at the bottom, looking as severe as she was able.

'What a mistake,' she said.

'You left us in the lurch there, said Ivar.

'Nothing I could do to help you,' said Mab. 'You've just had a little chat with Requin, the most terrible and powerful of all the magicians. There's nothing he doesn't know, no mischief he hasn't had a hand in, no conflict he isn't involved with. He sits up there with his devious mind working out his wicked schemes, quite regardless of the damage he may do.'

'Doesn't he care about anything?'

'He might, if he ever stopped to consider. But he was born a magician, the most gifted ever, they say. He was trained up by a great master, and there's nothing he can't do. So his mind is restless and complex, he loves to weave new webs. He is exceedingly dangerous, and I can't think why he let you into his room.'

'He knew who I was,' said Pebin.

'He knows who everyone is.'

'How could he know who I am?' said Scarlet. 'A

stranger from another world, he can't know me or anything about me.'

'Don't you be so sure,' said Mab, with a shake of her head.

Twenty-Nine

S HADOWS WERE LENGTHENING IN THE courtyards as they passed through one after another, linked by stone passages and stepped, arched ways. Scarlet's dreamlike day was becoming a nightmare again. Copper clouds were giving way to the sullen grey of an ill-omened night, and the light that sloped through the tiny-paned windows was grey and grim.

The gruffhound, flagging now, led them round another corner, into another tiny courtyard, where a fountain stood silent and lifeless in the centre. Wulfstan padded over to a small door which was set back from the wall through a pointed arch.

'Another magician's lair,' said Mab.

'No bones in there, I wouldn't think,' said Pebin at once. 'I vote we give it a miss.'

Ivar looked at the gruffhound, who had his nose pressed to the bottom of the door and was making excited snuffling noises. 'We do not,' he said. 'That looks to me like a hound that is on the scent.'

'Not necessarily bones, though,' pointed out Scarlet. 'More likely to be cat, or rats in the wainscoting.' She was rapidly losing faith in these bones. Time to give up the hunt, call it a day, pack up and go home.

Only she had no home, not until she found that door back to Juggler Street. And according to Natar, no prisoner, no door. No bones, no help from Ivar. No help from Ivar, no prisoner.

Ivar opened the door and wobbled through it. On the other side of it sat another magician. A kinder, sadder one, this time, and much older, in a cluttered, square room with little round windows. On his knees, he had a glowing crystal, and he looked up from it to gaze with weary eyes at the strange assortment of visitors to his chamber.

He was chanting to himself, as he glanced back down at the crystal; Scarlet strained to catch the words. The forces of Vemoria were on the move, the shadows of chaos and the Old Kings were rising, and his time, Tuan's time and the time of the castle was at its end.

Scarlet felt the hairs rise on the back of her neck, as the sadness and despair reached her. No, she told herself, resisting the dreadful sense of doom. It's not over yet, there's no use in just sitting and bewailing the end.

The sleek grey cat crouched on the back of his chair made a growling noise, and raised the fur along its back, as though in agreement with its master.

'Don't be so dreary,' said Mab. 'We aren't beaten yet.'

'It is written in the stars,' the man said in his melancholy way. 'Only magic of a kind that is no longer in our world could help us now. We are doomed. The Gods are heedless, we are their playthings, they mock us and make us their sport. It is finished.'

'Hooey,' said Mab. 'Here's an Otherworlder, arrived today. There's an indication that new possibilities are in the air.'

'A redhead, too,' said the magician with a gentle sigh. 'Like the boy who came to claim the Dewstone. Nothing came of that, he threw it away. She comes too late, and has no power, I fear; it is coincidence, all mere coincidence.'

'Oh, go and take some vitamins,' snapped Mab. 'I never heard anything so dismal. No bones in here, I suppose?'

'No, no bones,' said the magician, lapsing back into his coma of despair.

'I've no patience with it,' said Mab, stalking out. 'All these magicians and castle dwellers throwing in the towel at the first hint of trouble, what a useless lot. They've had it too easy for too long.'

Scarlet was thinking. 'Why do they all comment on my hair?'

Mab paused, looking shifty. 'It's an unusual colour, dear. And very striking.'

'Never mind her hair,' moaned Ivar. 'Where are my bones?'

Scarlet felt that the castle on that fateful evening was like a great building of state on the day war was declared, or perhaps at the end of a war, when hope and all the leaders had taken themselves off. It was like school after the end of term, with unfrequented passages and silent rooms. Or a railway station just before dawn, when even the station cat has settled down for a quiet half hour, and all trains are leaving; nobody arriving at all. It was as though the castle itself were brooding, casting melancholy shadows of doom and gloom along its passages and in its halls and stairways.

They came to an extraordinary room, with pillars like trees standing thickly across it in neat rows, stone arches like branches holding the roof above.

'The undercroft,' said Mab, wrapping her arms round herself as protection against the ancient chill.

'That means we're directly under the great hall; these pillars support the floor up there. Normally this place is bustling with life, goodness, what a depressing place it is right now. I'd rather be in the wild forest, or trapped in the swamp than here. I wish I'd never come.'

They stood among the twisted stone pillars, looking about them to see which way to go.

Scarlet heard footsteps coming up behind her, and whirled round to see who it was. 'Richard the Third,' she said with a shriek of laughter, as a man with a bent shoulder and a boar-embroidered jacket came up to them, moving like a large and ill-favoured spider.

The man with the crooked shoulder gave her an evil look. 'You're not the first Otherworlder to call me Richard Three, and I don't suppose you'll be the last,' he said.

'Huh, the way people round here are talking doom, I wouldn't be too sure,' said Ivar. He was so exhausted with all his fruitless enquiries that he didn't bother to beat about the bush. 'Listen, serf, I've lost my skeleton. Seen a set of bones anywhere?'

'And don't direct us to the graveyard,' said Pebin quickly. 'We've been there, done that.'

'Lost your bones?' said the man with an unwholesome leer. 'I'd try the lost-property cupboard, if I were you. Second floor, third passage on the left past the main stairs.'

With which cryptic words he scuttled on his way, leaving the four of them looking at each other doubtfully.

The gruffhound, defeated, had a good scratch.

'That's not very helpful,' said Pebin finally.

'It sounds unlikely,' said Scarlet. Although remembering her school lost-property cupboard, it wasn't impossible. The most extraordinary items did turn up in that.

'Where are the main stairs?' asked Ivar.

'That's a problem,' said Mab, a tiny frown wrinkling her usually smooth forehead. 'Main stairs? Castles don't have main stairs. Lots of little ones, yes. One or two bigger flights, like up from the kitchens to the great hall, yes. Broad stairways outside up to one of the upper entrances, okay. Do you suppose that crookback meant any of those?'

'No,' said Scarlet. She was thinking hard. 'But we did pass through what looked like a big gallery when we were on our way to the kitchens. Don't you remember? With stairs.'

Pebin, who was feeling more and more tired by the minute, made a great effort. 'She's right,' he said finally. 'And there was an imposing flight of stairs which led down off it.'

'It's worth a try,' said Mab.

'I know it's only my skeleton and my entire well-being we're talking about,' said Ivar huffily. 'Naturally, not worth making any effort over.'

'What have we been doing for the last goodness knows how many hours?' growled Pebin. He nudged Wulfstan with his toe. 'Come on, hound, give over with your fleas and find us the stairs.'

'Fleas!' said Ivar with disdain. 'Has it come to this?'

'Let's go and have a look,' said Scarlet. 'At least it'll pass the time until these forces of darkness tip up.'

'You could use your thoughtball,' suggested Pebin. 'To find the way.'

'Thoughtball?' exclaimed Ivar. 'This girl has a thoughtball, and never told us? Of course, you're making it up. Why should you have a thoughtball?'

'Well, I have.'

'With a thoughtball, we could have found my bones with no trouble at all.'

'No, we couldn't,' said Scarlet, 'a) because I'm not very good at using it; b) because we're in the castle, and I don't suppose it'd work, not with the clutter of magicians and so on that we've seen; and c) Natar told me only to try to use it in my hour of greatest need.'

'It may not be your hour of greatest need,' growled Ivar, 'but it is mine.'

'That's your problem,' said Scarlet, fingering the thoughtball in her pocket.

Thirty

*I*N THE END, THEY FOUND THE MAIN STAIRWAY entirely by accident. Pebin thought he heard a noise and went to investigate, and was knocked sideways down a narrow, half-visible passage by an enthusiastic gruffhound.

He told an unrepentant Wulfstan what he thought of him, and picked himself up. It was dark where he was, but he could see a light at the other end of the passage. Off he went to have a look, calling back to the others not to go on without him. He was back at the opening to the passage in seconds, shouting to the others to come and look.

'This isn't the stairway I had in mind,' said Mab.

'Maybe not,' said Pebin, 'but I bet it's the one we want.'

'There can't be a grander one than this in the castle,' said Scarlet. Just looking at it made her feel dizzy; never in her life had she seen such stairs. Wide enough for a dozen people to walk side by side, it ran up the walls of the huge round tower. Away from the wall, each tread had a fat barley-sugar column, with the twiddly bits picked out in gold. The row of twisted wooden pillars supported a gleaming banister rail the width of a tray.

'Kind of a spiral staircase,' Scarlet said. 'Winding round like that. Only at the side, holding on to the walls, not on a central pole. How does it stay up?' she added, peering up into the heights of the tower, where the stairway curved on up into the darkness.

'Magic,' said Mab. 'Don't fret about the stairs. We need to find the passage, and that cupboard.'

'Look,' said Pebin.

There was a tiny sign attached to the wall underneath the first curve of the staircase. Written on it in gothic script were the words Lost Property. A dagger pointed the way.

'Very practical,' said Ivar.

'Very unlikely,' said Mab suspiciously.

'Another sign,' said Scarlet, who was leading the way and had spotted it hanging from a hook at the next corner. 'Perhaps they lose a lot of things in the castle. So there'd be a lot of people needing the lost-property cupboard. It could be an important place.'

'I think not,' said Ivar, stopping in front of two closed doors which were framed by a low stone arch. Hanging on the large black handle on the left-hand door was a scrawled sign which said 'Lost Property. Gone to lunch. Back soon. Do not knock as there is nobody here.'

'Typical,' said Mab.

'Just like where I come from,' said Scarlet.

'I shall break the door down,' said Ivar. 'I shall hold it against Ril if my skeleton is in here. Such disrespect.'

'I wouldn't worry about that,' said Pebin. 'You'd be so pleased to get your bones back, you wouldn't care where they'd been.'

Mab was fiddling with the handle.

'What are you doing?' Ivar asked.

'Breaking and entering,' said Mab cheerfully. 'A witchy speciality. There are very few locks I can't pick, if I've got the time and I'm in the right mood.'

'And are you?'

'Yes,' said Mab, pleased with herself as she heard a click from inside the large lock. She grasped the handle, pushed it down, and gave a hefty tug at the door. 'Stiff,' she said.

With a few good heaves, the doors grudgingly opened, squeaking loudly.

'Rusty hinges,' said Mab. 'Doesn't look as though these doors have been open in a good while.'

'Deception,' said Ivar.

'It's very dark,' said Pebin.

'You can't tell what they've got in there.' Scarlet put out a hand to see what she could find. 'There's some kind of pole here.'

'A pikestaff,' said Pebin, skipping out of the way as the long-handled weapon fell to the ground with a loud clatter.

'There's a teapot,' said Mab, straining to see in the dark.

'Old boots,' said Scarlet rummaging around.

'Cushions,' said Pebin, fighting a cloud of feathers as the frayed fabric fell apart in his hands.

'A stuffed fish, look, it's horrible, its mouth's open and it's got a fearsome set of teeth.' This was better than any jumble sale, in Scarlet's opinion, although she couldn't see that there would be room for a set of bones.

'There's another door here,' said Pebin. 'By the side of the shelves.'

'Let me see.' Ivar forced himself forward, clutching his forehead with a decidedly limp hand. 'Ah,' he said. 'Aieee. Tingling. Pains, twinges, immortal agony, my bones must be here, I know they are.'

'Let me,' said Mab, pushing aside Ivar without ceremony. 'You're so floppy you couldn't open a pair of socks.'

'I'm overcome with weakness at the nearness of my bones, let me get at them.'

'All in good time,' said Mab and opened the cupboard.

'Hooray,' said Pebin.

'Woof,' said the gruffhound.

'I didn't know your bones were luminous,' said Scarlet, looking at the skeleton in admiration.

Mab reached into the cupboard and hauled the skeleton out. 'Try it for size,' she suggested to Ivar.

But Ivar had already seized the bones, and clasped them to himself, letting out yelps of pain and delight.

Before their eyes, the bones shimmered and dissolved into a pattern of tiny dots of light, and then the whole skeleton vanished. Ivar gave a final great shout, and then stood up straight, quite a head taller than before, punching the air above his head with glee.

Wulfstan crouched on the ground, paws drawn over his eyes.

'Ha,' said Ivar. 'I am a demigod again. Now, away from this terrible, sordid place. Ril will know of my discovery more quickly than he imagined.'

'Oy,' said Scarlet. 'Not so fast there. We have a deal, remember? We've found your bones, now you find the prisoner.'

'Deal?' Ivar waved a firm arm. 'We Immortals do not do deals with humans, or anyone else. Back to the Land of the Gods, to wreak my revenge.'

Thirty-One

*W*HILE EUPHORIA REIGNED OUTSIDE THE LOST-property cupboard, the forces of Vemoria were moving towards the Walled City in a sterner mode.

The group of black-clad horsemen weren't a big force, but any group of Vemorians carried terror with it. Unsettling terror, thought the people of Tuan as Uthar and his gang passed unchallenged across Tuan land.

Tuan wasn't in the least warlike.

'Vemorians? Funny lot, misguided; always up to something cruel,' was the general opinion.

Worries stirred in the heads of those who thought more. 'Remember last time, not so long ago, when they came pushing away our boundaries?'

'Yes, and captured villages, and took good Tuans as slaves.'

'Not all of them came back, either, when the boundaries were restored.'

Optimistic Tuans dismissed these fears. 'We did all right, then,' they insisted. 'It was just a little local difficulty. Nothing that guile and some good magic couldn't sort out, and will again.'

'We're all right, it's those Vemorians who should be fretting, what with those Twelve bullying them all.'

'Ah, but the Twelve have become one, and we Tuans should be ready for trouble.'

'He isn't bothering with us,' said a Tuan woman, peering out from behind closed shutters.

Her son, who had been hiding behind a wall as the troop went past, shot back into the house. 'Hundreds of horses, Ma. All with socks on.'

'Socks?' She stared. 'Get away with you.'

The boy dodged the slap for lying, and insisted he was speaking the truth. 'Honest, Ma. Black socks tied up over their hoofs. To muffle the sound, Jessem says.'

'And haven't I told you not to be out in the twilight with Jessem?' This time the slap got home. 'And hundreds of horses, indeed. No more than sixty.'

'Sixty Vemorians can do a lot of damage,' said her husband as he thumped down the wooden stairs. 'I reckon that Uthar's up to some special piece of wickedness. And when he's done that, why, he'll turn his attention to us. We aren't through with him yet, you mark my words.'

'Woe, woe,' said their son disrespectfully, as he went off to his bedchamber to look at the sullen moon which foretold, so people said, all manner of evil doings.

Thirty-Two

SCARLET WAS GLAD THAT MAB WAS THERE, TO quell Ivar's enthusiasm and direct his attention to other, urgent matters. Ivar reunited with his bones was an arrogant Ivar, still refusing to concern himself about finding the prisoner.

'Prisoner? I'm not interested in any prisoners. I told you, I'm going back to the Third Lands, to find Ril and give him grief.'

Mab wasn't having that. 'Ivar, you agreed.'

'No, I didn't,' said Ivar sulkily. 'I found the bones. I didn't need your help. I would have found them without you lot tagging along.'

'What a nerve!' cried Scarlet. 'Why, in your bendy state you couldn't even have opened the cupboard door. Even if you'd ever got to the cupboard, which isn't very likely.'

'Would so,' said Ivar.

'No, you wouldn't actually,' said Pebin. 'Not without us. And you said you'd help us once you'd found your bones.'

'No, I didn't. Or if I did, I didn't mean it.'

'Fingers crossed behind your back, I suppose,' said Scarlet.

'That's the one,' said Ivar. 'So you see, I'm leaving. If you're as good at finding things as you claim, you should have no trouble locating this prisoner.'

'Listen, buddy,' said Scarlet. 'We have no idea where he is or even what his name is. Only that he has red hair, and we'll recognize him, so Natar says.'

'Natar?' Ivar didn't seem to like the mention of Natar. 'Red hair, did you say? Well, if she's thinking about the same person I am, then forget it. That one's big trouble, and we Immortals aren't supposed to get mixed up in matters of state. Besides, there's nothing any of us could do if we found him. He's the only one who can end his imprisonment, and he won't do it.'

'What?' said Scarlet.

'And you'll recognize him? That's a good one.' He gave Scarlet a nasty look. 'I should think you would, too.'

''What do you mean by that?'

'If you don't know, I'm not telling you.' He folded his arms, turned his head away and began to whistle.

I really hate you, Scarlet said to herself.

'Don't fret,' said Mab. 'He's bound to help you, and he knows it. That's why he's being so peevish. He knows perfectly well that if he tried to walk away from the Walled City he'd have a bundle of Gods on to him like a ton of bricks. Losing his skeleton would be a trifle in comparison to what might happen to him.'

'Shut up, you horrible old witch,' hissed Ivar.

Mab took no notice. 'We need to find beds for the night,' she said. 'These two youngsters are exhausted, and I'm feeling very sleepy after all the excitement.'

'I thought all you witches were creatures of the night, hovering about getting up to mischief by the light of the moon,' grumbled Ivar.

'No moon tonight,' said Mab. 'And I dare say your bones are aching.'

They were, but Ivar wasn't going to admit it. 'Even a

demigod gets twinges now and again,' he said. 'And in this horrid damp castle, urgh!'

In the end, Requin found them rooms. He came walking out of the shadows, his face still in darkness. 'This way,' he said. 'Then tomorrow I will escort you from the castle.'

'We've ...' began Scarlet, but a look from Mab silenced her.

Requin stopped and smiled an icy smile. 'You were saying?'

'Oh, nothing,' she mumbled. 'Just that we'd be grateful.'

'Exactly so,' said Requin. He led the way up yet another flight of stairs to a passage lined with identical doors. A torch burned outside each one. 'Our guest quarters,' he said. 'You should find everything you need, and I do hope you'll be comfortable.'

Scarlet wanted one of the cell-like rooms to herself, but Mab was firm. 'There's a bigger one here, for two. We'll go in there.'

'Why?'

'Who knows what shadows roam the castle in the hours of darkness? Who knows what dreams Requin and his kind may weave up in those solitary chambers at the hour of the wolf, when the night has ended and the morning not yet begun?'

Mab stopped being poetic and became brisk. 'In here with me, and that's that.' She gave Scarlet a hefty shove; not such a softie, thought Scarlet as she flew across the vaulted bedchamber.

The beds were high, with ornately carved panels at head and foot. There was even a bathroom, 'like something out of ancient Crete,' said Scarlet, nearly vanishing down the immense plughole with the force of the shower.

'River water, stored in a tank,' said Mab. 'Make the most of it. As with the fountains, these will run dry. The water no longer flows, and it won't flow again until the balance is restored.'

'If it ever is,' said Scarlet, sliding into the chilly linen sheets of her bed. 'Wow, this is kind of luxurious.'

'Not what you're used to?' said Mab, who was sitting on the edge of her bed and teasing her hair into shape.

'Hardly.'

'Tsk, tsk,' said Mab. She waved a hand at the candles which lit the room and the flames died down at once.

'You missed those,' said Scarlet, fascinated. 'Over by that table.'

'We'll let them burn,' said Mab. 'The dark has its powers, and I don't think we need go asking for trouble. Goodnight.'

'Goodnight,' said Scarlet, and fell into a restless sleep.

Thirty-Three

'*E*EK,' SCREECHED SCARLET. SHE WAS HAVING A nightmare; a terrible dream, with this great black bird flapping at her.

'Wake up!' Someone was shaking her. Thankfully, Scarlet roused herself, and opened her eyes.

Eek again; there *was* a great black bird flapping about.

'Oh,' she said, diving back under the covers. 'It's you.'

The arpad jumped on to her bed, claws spread out, nearly breaking Scarlet's legs.

'Get off.'

'Do wake up,' said Mab.

Scarlet peered over the bedclothes once more. 'You're up. Dressed!' She noticed the candles were still burning, although they were guttering low in their holders now. 'Is it morning yet? It's very dark.'

'Dawn,' said Mab. 'And we have to be on the move, we're not waiting for Requin. I've woken the others, so get up as fast as you can, no time to spare.' She dived into a big black closet which Scarlet hadn't noticed before. 'Ah,' she said, pulling out an armful of dark material. 'Cloaks. It will be cold where we're going.'

Scarlet wanted to argue. She demanded an explanation, information, but Mab wasn't having any of it. 'We can talk once we're on our way.'

'There'll be guards,' said Scarlet. 'If Requin doesn't want us to go without him.'

'Ivar's dealt with them,' said Mab. 'Hurry.'

Less than ten minutes later they were creeping down a stone spiral staircase. Without the arpad, who had let herself out into one of the open courtyards, saying they would meet outside the castle, on the way to the mountains.

'Mountains?' said Scarlet, bemused. 'What mountains?'

'Sssh,' said Pebin.

'Quiet,' said Mab.

'Shut up,' said Ivar, who seemed very alert and lively, and was leading the way with great striding steps. Obviously a rest had restored his bones.

'I'll see to the gatekeeper, if he's around,' said Ivar with a flash of malice in his voice. 'Especially if it's Querle.'

Luckily for Querle, it wasn't. Instead, it was a dumpy little fellow who peered out at them through the grille with bleary eyes.

Ivar leant against the door, there was a splintering sound and it swung open, sending the gatekeeper flying. Ivar scooped him up.

'His wife will get a shock when she finds him in that great stone jar, come the morning,' said Mab.

'She'll find him long before that, the noise he's making,' said Scarlet.

Pebin was worried. 'Won't they raise the alarm?'

'No way,' said Mab. 'He'd only get into trouble for not stopping us. No, she'll get him out of the jar and tick him off and make him go back to bed. People like that know it's best to keep their heads down at times like these.'

Pity we don't, thought Scarlet as they made their way

through dark and deserted streets. The faint light of dawn was enough for them to see where they were going, but it was a chill and cheerless light, promising no good for the day to come.

'Out at the Eastern Gate,' said Ivar.

'Why?' said Pebin.

'It's the nearest, and it's the one they never close. Once we're outside the city, their magic is weakened. Of course it's not a problem for me, there's nothing they can do to me. I can just skip home to the Third Lands whenever I like. And I suppose you have some witchy nest,' he said nastily to Mab. 'As for these two, well, no hope for them unless we get them clear.'

As they passed through the gate the shadowy figure of the arpad flew down from the sky to join them.

'Faster,' said Beak One.

'They're doomed,' said Two.

'Very helpful,' said Scarlet. 'What's up? Why are we heading for the mountains? Which mountains? And why in this hugger-mugger way?'

'We were watching the castle,' said Beak One. 'Last night.'

'A messenger left, at great speed,' said Two.

'We followed. He crossed into south Tuan.'

'And met up with Uthar and his troop.'

'Uthar on the move, huh?' put in Ivar.

'We listened,' said Beak One.

'I listened,' said Two. 'You never hear whispers clearly.'

'They weren't whispering. Quite brazen they were. The messenger . . .'

'. . . came from Requin. He offered . . .'

'. . . to hand you, Scarlet, over to Uthar, if Uthar agreed to leave the castle alone.'

'Me?' said Scarlet. 'Why me?'

The arpad nodded both its heads. 'You,' said One. 'He doesn't like Otherworlders, Uthar doesn't.'

'Never has,' agreed Two.

'It seems that Uthar's known you were here since you came through,' said Mab.

'I can't imagine how,' said Scarlet, not liking the sound of that at all.

'He has spies everywhere,' said Pebin, who was feeling cold and sleepy and miserable, and wondering if his parents would have enough of their powers left to know where he was. If not, and if he ever got back in one piece, it would be Big Trouble.

'Not for the first time,' said Mab consolingly.

'This Uthar must be mad. And how come Requin knows that Uthar's after me?'

'Requin knows everything he needs to, and a lot he doesn't.'

'And?'

'It was easy for his devious mind to work out what a good bargaining point you are. So he made the offer to Uthar. An offer that Uthar accepted, on the spot. No quibbles, no questions, according to what the arpad says.' Mab sighed. 'Really, I'm out of my depth with all this.'

Scarlet didn't make any noble suggestions about the others abandoning her for their own safety. She might be the quarry, although she didn't altogether buy that, but it wasn't in her nature to give in to bullies. This Uthar sounded a Grade A bully. 'So now we'll have both of them after me?' she said astutely. 'Requin, so that he can hand me over to Uthar, and Uthar himself.'

'An unpleasant predicament,' said Ivar.

'I still don't see why Uthar's bothered about me,' said Scarlet.

'You will,' said Ivar.

'I'm hungry,' said Pebin. 'Is there any food left? And why are we heading for the mountains?'

'Oh, didn't I say?' said Ivar carelessly. 'That's where the prisoner is. And it's the prisoner Uthar really wants so perhaps we'd better go and winkle him out first. If Natar says that's what we have to do.'

'Do you know exactly where he is?'

'No, not precisely. No doubt the thoughtball can help us.'

'Don't count on it.' Scarlet's sleepy brain was trying to wrap itself round this story. 'Does Uthar want me *and* the prisoner? Why does he think getting hold of me will give him the prisoner? Exactly who is this prisoner, in any case?'

'The last of the Old Kings,' said Ivar with a yawn. 'Merleon. Terrible nuisance that he didn't get sent out of time with all the others, and I say that although he's a friend of mine. He can give Uthar access to the old wild magic, and that would complete Uthar's power.'

Pebin, too, was thinking hard. 'If the prisoner can use the old magic, how come he hasn't? I mean, why is he still a prisoner?'

'Scruples,' said Ivar with a curl of his lip. 'Doesn't want to let that particular genie out of the lamp again. If he uses the old wild magic to free himself – and you're right, he could do that whenever he wants – then it's out for good, and the whole power of the Old Kings will start to rise again.'

'What's wrong with the old magic?' asked Scarlet.

Pebin knew about that. 'It's destructive,' he said at once. 'It's uncontrollable and anarchic. When that's around, you never know where you are. No orderly life, no cities, no laws, no trade, just chaos.'

'Can see you listen to some of your lessons,' said Ivar. 'Swot. Yes, Merleon knows that the wild magic would mean the end of life in Vemoria and Tuan and the Gonelands as it is today. He doesn't want to be a king, says the time of the Old Kings is past. Bit pathetic, really, with all that power at his fingertips.' Ivar flexed his own strong fingers, admiring their bony shape.

'All very well,' said Scarlet, 'but why me?'

'Uthar thinks Merleon will do anything to save you,' said Mab sharply. 'And he's probably right.' She pulled the cloak she had taken out of the castle closet more closely round her.

'Merleon doesn't know me.'

Ivar gave a contemptuous snort. 'He doesn't have to.'

'Why not?'

'He'll recognize you as soon as he claps eyes on you!'

'It doesn't seem very likely. Why should he?'

Ivar gave a wicked laugh. 'Because you're his daughter, that's why!'

Thirty-Four

CULUN HAD VOICED HIS DOUBTS ABOUT UTHAR'S plan before Uthar set off for the Walled City. 'Will Merleon do as you think he will?'

'Yes.'

'Break out, do what you want, use the wild magic, let it loose once more? Just to save a daughter he's never met?'

'Yes.'

'Would you?'

'No, but I'm not lily-livered.'

Erica wasn't with them; Erica was minding the shop back in Vemoria. Her father's callous words wouldn't have disturbed her, had she heard them. She had the same ruthlessness herself. You didn't give in for the sake of *any* individual. When the time came, when she was older, and Uthar's rule lay heavy on him, when he was tired from years of control, then she'd boot her father out. Just as he'd booted out the other eleven of the Twelve. That was natural. That was how history worked; the weak yielding to the strong.

'Merleon is weak,' said Uthar with contempt.

Culun scratched the side of his nose with a chubby finger, a sign that he was thinking hard.

'He's had it all within his grasp,' Uthar went on. 'Tuan, the Walled City, the castle even. And Vemoria, too. And what did he do? Drift into the other world, pretend to be a normal person, shun and deny the forces of the old kingdom which were his from birth.' Uthar's eyes gleamed with power lust. 'Such amazing power. Unlimited. In his hands. What a fool he is!'

'We still don't know where he is.'

'No, but Requin does. Requin will hand over this girl, and tell us where her father is. Then it's up to us.' He paused. 'It's turned out for the best that we didn't capture her in the other world, as we tried to. She's much more use to us over here, And who knows, she's her father's daughter, we may even get our hands on the Dewstone through her. As a bonus.'

'If Merleon lets loose the old magic, what use is the Dewstone?'

'A little extra insurance,' said Uthar evilly.

He was much less pleased with the state of affairs some two hours later. He strode into Requin's chamber, smiling with a smile that reached no further than the ends of his mouth – and that was making an effort.

'The girl?' he said.

'It is customary to knock.'

'Knock?'

'On the door.'

'Oh, never mind that. The girl, hand over the girl.'

Requin looked at Uthar with distaste. Even for one of his wily ways, it was unpleasant to do business with such a man. 'She isn't here,' he said, rising from his seat and throwing some powder on the fire. It gave off a shower of green sparks and then hissed sullenly with little spurts and tongues of red and blue flames, which cracked and flickered, sending eerie patterns of light and shadow dancing round the walls of the room.

Uthar exploded. Black ill-will streamed out of him, causing Requin's cat to leap, spitting and growling, from its cushion and take up residence on the broad shelf above the fire.

Requin raised a hand, and Uthar stopped dead in his tracks. He gasped, as though he had been punched in the stomach.

'What was that? Why did you do that?'

'I just sent your temper and anger back towards you,' said Requin. 'Don't ever do that again, Uthar. Now listen to me. The girl has left the castle.'

'Left the castle? *Left*?' His rage about to boil over again, he saw Requin's hand twitch and controlled himself. 'Why did you let her go?'

'I have not, at the moment, the manpower I need. Because of your very obvious tramping across Tuan, and because of some strange weather and so forth, the idiotic people who work in the castle have bolted and taken cover outside our walls. Natar – you remember Natar? – has kept everyone here well informed of what is happening in Vemoria; she's to blame for much of this.'

'Natar!' said Uthar, in a voice full of hatred.

'A thorn in all our sides,' said Requin.

'I'll deal with her when I hold Tuan,' said Uthar evilly. Then he returned to his main grievance. 'You don't need much manpower to keep hold of a girl.'

'She is no ordinary girl,' Requin reminded him.

'She has no powers.'

'Of course she has. She doesn't know it yet, but she will. And I'm risking no confrontations with a descendant of the Old Kings here in this place.'

'This place! There will be no this place. I'll raze the castle to the ground, I'll take all you magicians and . . .'

'Not if you want the girl, you won't.'

'You haven't got the girl.'

'No, but I know where she is. And I know where she's going.'

'Then tell me, and I'll be off.'

'First,' said Requin, 'we'll make sure that our arrangement is binding. I wouldn't want you to find the girl, and then her father, and then forget what you owed me, and your promise about the castle.'

'If I want to attack the Walled City, I shall. As ruler of Vemoria and Tuan, I can have no focus of discontent in my territories. No sorcerers, no soothsayers, no anybody who doesn't work for me.'

'The Walled City you may do as you wish with. That is not our magic, it is Tuan magic. As a matter of fact, at the moment the Tuans have no magic to speak of. The balance is gone, and their skills with it. The fountains have stopped flowing, the channels are dry, I doubt if they'd be able to resist you. But the castle, which as you know is older by far than the city, and which draws its magic from a different source, that, Uthar, you will leave alone.'

'Oh, very well,' said Uthar ungraciously. 'I suppose so.'

'You will pay with your life and all your lands, if you try to break our bond.'

'Huh,' said Uthar, and then recoiled as he felt dagger pains curling round his heart. 'Yes, okay, all right. It's binding. I agree. Now tell me where the girl is.'

Thirty-Five

*I*T WAS PEBIN WHO NOTICED THEY WERE BEING followed, and the arpad who confirmed it.

'What's up?' Scarlet asked, still yawning her head off from the early start.

Pebin rubbed the back of his head. 'I've got this feeling. I think there's someone behind us.'

Ivar swung round and looked back towards the city, red and grey under skies which were still heavy with purple and copper clouds. 'I can't see anyone.'

'It's not so much see,' said Pebin, 'as feel. Know.'

'We'll look, we'll search,' said the arpad, taking off with a great feathery whirr of her strong wings.

'Mab?' said Scarlet, nudging Mab, who seemed to be in a dream. 'Mab?'

'Eh?' said Mab, startled. 'Yes? What is it?'

'You didn't hear what Pebin said. He feels we're being followed.'

'Then we probably are,' said Mab. 'In fact, of course we are. Requin must know we've gone. He's not one to let us get away without him knowing what we're doing and where we're going.'

'Then what's the point?' burst out Scarlet, her voice shrill with fear. 'He'll simply scoop us up and take us back to the castle.'

'Scoop?' said Ivar. 'Scoop? *Me*? He will not. Me, a demigod, an Immortal?'

'Keep your hair on,' said Scarlet.

'He's following us so that he can find out where Merleon is.'

Scarlet looked mutinous. She didn't want to hear any more of this Merleon. Her father? No way. What a load of hooey; she'd never heard anything so stupid in her life, she'd told Ivar so when he made his revelation. 'My father lives near London; he moved there when he left my mum. He's married to someone else, and they've got a son. He's English. Lives in England. Always has. Okay?'

'The likeness is unmistakable.'

'That's really stupid. How old is this guy? Years and years older than I am, and he's a man. We're hardly going to be identical twins. Lots of people look similar to other people who are no relation at all.'

Ivar was unconvinced. 'You have a look to you.'

'Red hair, that's all,' said Scarlet. 'Big deal. Pebin's got red hair.'

'Not the same kind,' said Mab. 'Don't get worked up about it, Scarlet. Although it is odd, your coming through. Looking as you do. And just at this particular time.'

'Coincidence. An accident, that's all. And I'll be gone as soon as I can, and it won't be a moment too soon.'

'Don't you want to find Merleon?'

Scarlet raised her chin. 'You say he's my father, I say he's not. I care about him because he's my ticket home. But he's only a name to me, I don't know him, I've never met him, and all this about Old Kings and wild magic isn't any part of my world.'

'If he's your father, then it is,' said Pebin.

'If, only he isn't. My mum, married to one of these Old Kings? Come on, it doesn't sound very likely, does it? Besides, this Merleon guy sounds a real creep. He's a

—— 144 ——

prisoner who could escape any time he wanted, only he doesn't want to. While people get thrown down oubliettes and so on, all because of him. I've no patience with anybody like that. Sounds as though he ought to be in a home.'

Scarlet was still feeling angry with Ivar and his irritating certainty that he knew better than she did who she was. It was maddening. And now here was the gruffhound growling and making little barking noises in the back of his throat; what had he found?

'He's barking at the mountains,' said Mab.

'Silly dog,' said Scarlet, ruffling the back of his neck. To her surprise, to everyone's surprise, he sprang away from her, giving her a quick bite on the way, and stood a short distance away from her, growling in a very menacing way, tail tucked between his legs.

She took a step forward, her hand outstretched. 'Hey, gruffhound, Wulfstan, what's all this about?'

The growling changed to full volume and very threatening barking.

'Be careful,' said Pebin. 'Don't go near him, Scarlet, you can see he's ready to fly at you. I wonder what's annoyed him.'

Mab took a handful of loose gruffhound neck in her hand and dragged him further away, to a safer distance from Scarlet. 'Go, hound. Take your way, find your master.'

And the gruffhound, after a moment's hesitation, gave a final loud bark and set off with great loping strides back towards the city.

Scarlet was sorry to see him go, and puzzled by his behaviour. 'How come a dog's bothered by mountains?'

'Not just the mountains, although these are strange mountains, but by what's in them. Let him go. He's done his work for us, and I expect Hoebe's been out all night looking for him. He loves that dog.'

Wulfstan's strange behaviour and speedy departure lowered their spirits. They walked on in silence, following a well-marked track which climbed steadily towards the line of mountains.

'It's a long way,' said Pebin at last.

'It isn't as far as it looks,' said Mab. 'With these mountains, one minute they're on the horizon, and the next minute you're there, in the foothills.'

Pebin didn't think that very likely, but there was no point in arguing about it.

Scarlet, raising her eyes for a moment from the ground, which she was resolutely staring at as she walked, saw a shape wheeling in the sky. 'The arpad,' she cried.

'Bother,' said Beak One, as she made a none-too-good landing on the steep path.

'Arpads like level ground,' said Two, fluffing out her feathers.

'What news?' said Ivar. 'Does Requin dare to send minions after us?'

'Not exactly minions,' said Beak One.

'No, more like those sharp little creatures that hang around magicians. From the forests, you know the ones.'

'Forest-dwellers?' Mab didn't like the sound of that. 'And where are they?'

'Tracking,' said One.

'Keeping two or three hundred paces behind you. They could close, any time they wanted.'

What was wrong with forest-dwellers? Scarlet wanted to know.

Mab gave a gusty sigh. 'They hardly ever stray outside the darkest parts of the forests. They have their own ways and tracks through the forest, which none but they can use. They shadow travellers making journeys along the main paths and if one of them should stray to either side . . .'

'Kaput,' said Pebin dramatically. 'Never seen again, isn't that right, auntie?'

'What, they kill them?' Scarlet was shocked. 'Dangerous places, your forests.'

'Nobody knows for sure,' said Mab, wringing her hands. 'They say that the forest-dwellers keep them. To work for them. They also say that their captives go mad, since the forest is thick with panic fear. They say that then the dwellers let them loose and they wander wailing and screaming amid the darkness of the trees.'

'Sound like bogey tales to me,' said Scarlet, refusing to give in to the lurching panic which made her want to be anywhere but where she was. 'Nasties to frighten the children. Horror videos. Anyway, if these forest-dwellers hang about waiting to get up to mischief in the forests, why should they be here, prowling around after us? I see no trees.'

'Ah, that's the cunning of Requin,' said Mab.

'He's got a great deal too big for his boots, that man,' said Ivar loftily. 'When I get back home I'm going to have a word with one or two friends about him. He isn't safe.'

'Requin recruits all sorts who live on the edge,' said Mab. 'The ones who don't belong, people of the forests, of the night, of the high mountains. He weaves a web of magic about them, and they become his daemons.'

'What?' said Scarlet. 'Are you serious?'

'Wait and see,' said Ivar. 'Of course, the forest-dwellers can't touch me, being what I am.'

'Hum,' said Mab.

'I can't breathe,' said Pebin, by and by. 'Do we have to go at this speed?'

'We're climbing fast,' said Mab.

'No problem for me,' said Ivar, taking deep breaths to demonstrate his superiority.

'Show-off,' said Scarlet, who, like Pebin, was finding herself more and more short of breath. Not that she was going to admit it.

Mab was right. In less time than seemed possible, the trees and greenery of further down were left behind, and the path became even steeper, winding its way through great rocks and boulders.

'Looks as though someone's tossed them here,' said Scarlet.

'They did,' said Ivar. 'Aeons ago, when the Gods fought their first great battles.'

A likely story, thought Scarlet, but she didn't have the energy to argue. Every step was becoming painful, every stretch of path covered was an achievement.

Mab didn't seem bothered at all. 'We witches aren't,' she said. 'We're creatures of air, when we want to be. I have all sorts of friends and acquaintances living in high places, it's not a problem.'

'Ivar,' said Scarlet, very slowly, so as to conserve her breath. 'How far have we to go? Where is this guy kept?'

'Ah,' said Ivar. 'I'm glad you asked me that. He's in these mountains, that I do know. I can be sure of that. You don't have to have any doubts about that at all.'

'We don't,' said Mab, looking at Ivar with a very severe expression. 'Do go on.'

'Ah, well you see, it's a matter of exactly *where* he is in these mountains.'

'Yes?'

'Um.'

'Um?' panted Scarlet.

'Um?' echoed Pebin, coughing hard.

'Um, I don't know,' said Ivar, with a careless flourish of his hand.

Thirty-Six

'I RECKON,' SAID PEBIN, 'THAT THIS IS THE TIME to use the thoughtball.'

Scarlet was furious. 'Oh, great. I can't even breathe, and you're suggesting I have a go with the thoughtball. What a good idea, why didn't I think of it? Listen, last time, I had a range of halfway across the room, and then crash. How far away is this Merleon likely to be?'

'Further than that,' said Mab. 'But you don't need breath to use a thoughtball.'

Scarlet dug deep into her pocket, and pulled out the shining black globe. As she rubbed it with the palm of her hand, the lights began to sparkle.

'Pretty,' said Ivar.

Scarlet held it out to Mab. 'You use it. You're a witch, it'll be a doddle for you.'

'Sadly, not,' said Mab. 'We witches do not command the great magic.'

'Great magic? Old magic? Wild magic? What is all this crazy stuff? What magic do you do, then? I mean, I've seen you turn yourself into other things, just like that.' She snapped her fingers in the air.

'Witchy magic,' said Mab firmly. 'Quite a different order of things.'

'Well, it's still more than you can expect of me,' said Scarlet indignantly. 'I'm not into any kind of magic. I haven't been to school to learn it, like Pebin, have I?'

She turned to Ivar. 'Go on, you use it. You obviously rank high, if you're immortal. You send it off to find Merleon.'

'Sorry,' said Ivar, not sounding in the least bit sorry. He shook his golden curls to emphasize the point. 'I don't do thoughtballs. Impossible. Not in my line at all.'

'You could try,' said Scarlet. 'I thought you were a friend of his, don't you want to help him?'

'He doesn't seem to want to help himself.'

'Only because he doesn't want to let loose the old magic,' said Mab.

Ivar shrugged. 'That's his problem, but it makes no difference. Demigods and thoughtballs do not go together.'

'It's up to you,' Mab said to Scarlet. 'It's worth a go; if you can't do it, then we're no worse off than we are now.'

'Bet you can do it,' said Pebin suddenly. 'Bet you'll be able to make it work out here. It's different here from Natar's place.'

'Yes, like in Natar's place I could breathe.'

'Try,' urged Mab.

Scarlet looked at the three of them. Mab's face was friendly, but gave nothing away. Pebin had a pleading look on his face. Ivar just looked cunning.

'Okay.'

She went over to a rock which had, she'd already noticed, a slight dip in its centre. She put the thought-ball into the shallow indentation, and stood back to look at it.

'It's humming,' said Pebin. 'Listen. And masses of lights. I think it's going to work. Can you remember what he looked like, Scarlet? You need to keep that in your mind.'

Scarlet nodded, never taking her eyes off the ball. 'If

it does get up and go,' she hissed, 'how do we know where it's gone? It shot off, the one Natar sent.'

'You make it go slowly,' said Mab. 'Then we follow it.'

'*Make* it? Huh.'

Scarlet took as deep a breath as she could, and tried to remember how it had felt back there in Natar's room. Her head spun, there was a ringing in her ears, dizziness crept up her spine. Must think of the picture, she told herself. Concentrate on the man in the picture.

And then the haze behind her eyes cleared, and the thoughtball was hovering above the rock, sparkling as it spun gently round. Scarlet drew it higher, and then sent it on its way for all the world as though she had given it a soft pat with a tennis racquet.

'Hey, look at that,' said Pebin.

'Remarkable,' said Ivar.

'Off we go,' said Mab.

Scarlet's breathlessness had disappeared, and she felt light-headed and exhilarated. The scenery around her, the rocks and boulders, the patches of grass and the towering crags and peaks above them had a clarity and sharpness to them that she had never seen before. As though they had just been made, she thought, with the part of her mind that wasn't focused on the man in the picture and keeping the thoughtball aloft.

'Bet Ivar buzzes off now,' Pebin whispered to Mab, as they made their way up a narrow track.

'Not him,' said Mab. 'He's far too nosy, he's itching to know how things turn out. Then he can go back to the Third Lands and talk about it. All these demigods are tremendous gossips.'

'It does seem to know where it's going, the thought-ball,' Pebin said a few minutes later, as they came to a fork, and the black ball zoomed off up the steeper, narrower, rougher track. 'Are you sure it isn't a will-o'-the-wisp, leading us into the marshes?'

'Pebin!' said Mab. 'I'm ashamed of you, and you a Tuan of the Walled City. You know what thoughtballs are and what they can do.'

'Yes, but maybe Scarlet can't control it properly. Usually it's only the oldies who get to use them, and that's after years and years of practice. I never heard of anyone young managing a thoughtball.'

'Ssh,' said Mab. 'Scarlet's doing fine, just fine. Keep going, you can see it's leading us somewhere.'

'Yes, but where?'

'We'll find out shortly.'

'And we're still being followed,' said Pebin after another pause. 'I think they're closer.'

'We could ask the arpad, if she hadn't flapped off again,' said Mab.

Pebin searched the turbulent skies with keen eyes.

'There's the arpad,' he said. 'Way up.'

'Wave,' said Mab, waving furiously herself. 'With two pairs of eyes, she must see us.'

'Yes, but then the two heads will start arguing with each other about whether we're waving to them or to someone else, and whether it means she should come down or not.'

It did look as though the arpad was having a quick discussion with herself, but by the time Mab and her party had got over or round the next batch of boulders, the huge bird was making a descent, circling down from the sky in a series of hiccupy loops.

'Terrible turbulence up there,' said One.

'Air currents,' said Two.

'Are those forest horrors still on our tail?' Pebin asked.

'Yes, and closing. They can move much faster than

you, nasty little things, whipping along the ground like rats.'

'Rats? I thought they were the size of small people.'

'Big rats,' said Two.

Thirty-Seven

*T*HEY WENT ON AND UP, THE PATH NOW GREY
and dusty underfoot, almost volcanic, Scarlet
thought, although it didn't bother her; all her energies
were for the thoughtball.

Which was starting to behave oddly.

They were climbing up a particularly stiff and steep
part of the path which led them through a narrow gully
with sheer rock towering above them on either side.
Doesn't like being shut in, thought Scarlet, but no, it
was more than that.

To begin with, it was just a series of slight zigzags.

Concentrate, Scarlet told herself.

Then it made a zinging noise, which crescendoed
into a series of wails. They rang across the mountains in
a very noticeable way, alarming them all.

'Can't you stop it doing that?' said Pebin, aware of
how close on their heels the forest-dwellers were.

'No,' said Scarlet, who was puzzled by the thoughtball's antics, but could do nothing about them.

Then the ball shot up into the air, down again, cut a
few fancy loops, hovered for a second or two . . . and
whoosh! it was gone.

Ivar bounded up the path to look over the ridge
which would lead them on to the next agonizing ascent.
He waved at the others to join him.

They looked down, not on to another path and

another climb, but into an idyllic green valley. Lush grass grew beside a stream that meandered along the bottom, trees in every shade of green grew up the slopes. And there, beside the stream, was a glass dome.

'Not exactly glass,' Pebin said finally. 'It's like a marble.'

And it was, with threads of colour, blue and green and gold, seemingly caught between bubbles of air frozen in the curved arch of glass.

'Merleon's home?' asked Scarlet.

'Yes,' said Mab. 'There's the thoughtball, down there, beside it.'

'There's no door on this side,' said Pebin.

'And probably none on the other, either,' said Ivar.

'There must be an entrance of some kind.' Scarlet was definite. 'He has to have food and so on.'

'There are creatures which can travel through this kind of glass.'

'Arpads,' said Beaks One and Two simultaneously.

'Off you go,' said Mab.

'He'll be pleased to see us,' said One, as she soared into the air.

'Don't you depend on it,' said Two. 'He might be thinking great thoughts, not happy to be interrupted.'

'Thinking about his breakfast if he's got any sense,' said One, with a raucous laugh.

'Cackle, cackle,' said Two. 'That's all you're good for.'

The arpad was cackling on the other side of her faces when she flapped back to land at Ivar's feet. The others were sitting down, eating the last of the food that Mab had brought with her from the castle.

'Tough glass,' said One.

Two snatched a piece of bread from under Pebin's nose.

'Hey,' said Pebin.

'Hard work, going through glass like that,' said Two, with its mouth full.

'How can you go through glass?' said Scarlet.

'It's like mist to us,' said One. 'We come from another plane, and there glass is a liquid.'

'Are there any doors?'

'No,' said Two, still chewing. 'Bit stale, this bread.'

'It's yesterday's,' said Mab. 'No way in or out?'

'No. Smooth and unbroken all the way round.'

'Someone must get in there,' said Scarlet.

'Do they count as someones, the Thinlings?' said One.

'More like somethings, in my opinion. They give me the shudders.'

'Thinlings?' Even Pebin hadn't heard of them. 'Worse than the forest-dwellers?' he asked nervously, looking over his shoulder as he spoke.

'Different,' said Ivar. 'And very unexpected, in these parts.'

'They're like stick insects,' said Mab. 'They skip about the place and skitter here and there; you can never get any sense out of them.'

'What's interesting about them,' said Ivar, 'is that they come from the other side of the Land of the Gods. What are they doing here? Who sent them? What keeps them here, so far from home?'

'Requin?' said Scarlet.

Neither Ivar nor Mab thought that likely.

'Not his style,' said Mab.

'He would have no power over Thinlings,' said Ivar.

'What are these Thinlings for?'

'They'll look after Merleon. Your father,' added Ivar, just to annoy.

'He must have company, someone to talk to.'

'Did he speak to you?' Pebin asked the arpad.

'He didn't notice us,' said One.

'Didn't notice you?' Scarlet wondered how you could not notice an arpad.

'He was asleep,' said Two.

'They're getting nearer,' said Pebin, peering nervously over the top of the slope where they were sitting and looking down at the steep path below. There was no one to be seen, but he knew the forest-dwellers were there.

'Hiding in the shadows,' said Mab. 'Look, there's one.'

Scarlet looked, but could only see stones and rocks.

'I'll deal with them,' said Ivar, having a good stretch and flexing his muscles. Now he had grown back into his bones he was about seven feet tall. Short for a demigod, Mab said, but he looked large enough to Scarlet.

Ivar stood on the top of the ridge. There was a boulder, one of those that looked as though it had landed there in some celestial ball game. Unattached, and not grown in, it was balanced against a rocky outcrop.

Ivar was beside it, pursing his lips, and tapping his mouth with his fingers. Then he bent, and heaved, and the boulder danced across the hillside and bounced and rolled down the path they had just come up, and into the narrow gully, blocking it completely.

'Ha,' said Ivar. 'That'll hold them up for a while.'

Thirty-Eight

*B*EHIND THE FOREST-DWELLERS, AND travelling fast, was Uthar and his troop.

Behind Uthar and his troop, but keeping well out of sight, was Requin. As he had left the castle and stalked out of the city, those still abroad wondered and whispered. No one remembered seeing the great magician leave his lair – not by daylight, at any event.

'Course, he's all over the place come the night,' said one citizen.

'That cat of his turns into a dragon, and he rides out of time on it.'

'No, he stays in time, wants to know everything that's going on, Requin.'

'He could do that just by sitting in his chamber and casting a few runes.'

'Needs his exercise, like anyone else.'

Behind Requin came Erica, accompanied by a reluctant Culun.

'I should be in Vemoria. A country with no one at its helm is a country in danger.'

Erica had blazed out at him for that. 'Do you suggest that the country is not totally under my father's command?'

Silence.

'Well?'

'Of course it is, but . . .'

'But nothing. His men are in place, the watchers have been doubled, the curfew extended. Nothing can happen in Vemoria while Uthar is away. And as for you, you could go on holiday for three months, and it wouldn't make any difference. In fact,' she went on, 'I shall recommend that my father sends you off on holiday. A *long* holiday. A few weeks in a health farm, I think; it would do wonders for your waistline.'

'As you say.' Culun bowed his head.

'I do say. Get a move on.'

'Why are we going?' Culun waited for a torrent of criticism at his daring to ask, but Erica considered that a sensible question.

'I've had news from the Otherworld.'

'Can that affect your father's plans?'

'Nothing can do that,' said Erica. 'But he may need this information, and there's no one I can trust with it. Besides, I want to be there when he gets the better of Merleon and makes him bow to his wishes.'

'Just so,' said Culun with another nod of his head.

Thirty-Nine

*I*N THE OTHERWORLD, WHILE SCARLET HAD BEEN walking down the street and going through the door under the archway, Ben had been on his travels.

Terrestial travels, this time, not like his last great journey, when he had vanished in the mist and crossed the boundary into another world, to find himself wandering alone in the snowy Third Lands. He hadn't known he was the long-awaited Red One, but friends and foe alike had recognized that flaming red hair, and knew that he had come to claim the Dewstone.

His mother was going away for a few days. 'You'll only miss the last couple of days of school if you go down to your aunt,' she said.

'It's not missing school I mind,' said Ben. 'It's my aunt. Nettle soups, and funny weeds from the garden on your plate.'

'Not at this time of year.' Ben's mum was apologetic, but she couldn't leave Ben alone in the flat for all that time.

'I know,' said Ben. 'Couldn't I go and stay with Hal and Gilly?'

'Oh, Ben, you hardly know them. They're older than you, for one thing. I can't just ring up and ask if you can go and stay.'

'All right,' said Ben. 'I'll ring them.'

It was quickly settled. Ben's mum was so relieved that

Ben had somewhere to go and felt happy about it that she enquired no further.

'I think Hal and Gilly are really lucky,' Ben said that evening at tea-time. 'Being two of them. I think it's tough, being an only child.' Then he saw the look on his mother's face. 'Sorry, Mum, I didn't mean it. If Dad hadn't gone off like that, perhaps you would have had more children. I don't mind, not really.'

'Why did you say it, then?'

'I have this dream,' Ben said. 'Sometimes, and a lot just recently. I dream that I've got an older sister. With red hair. A bit wild.'

Ben's mum tried to laugh. 'Ben, you'd hate having an older sister. She'd boss you about.'

'I suppose so,' said Ben.

That hadn't been the end of it, and as he got off the coach, he was longing to tell Hall and Gilly his news. They'd both come to meet him, standing by the bay where the coach drew in, jumping up and down to keep out the cold wind.

'Mum's round the corner,' said Gilly.

'Jolly wise, staying in the car,' said Hal.

'Thank you for meeting me,' said Ben.

He wanted to tell them his news right away, but as soon as they got back to Gilly and Hal's house, he was roped in to help with the Yule log.

'It's special, Ben,' Gilly said.

'Made from the root of an apple tree that came from Vemoria,' added Hal.

'Vemoria?' Ben didn't have very good memories of Vemoria.

'Not Vemoria now; old Vemoria. It grew from a seed Gilly picked up in the orchard of the Old Kings,' said Hal.

'We didn't realize we'd brought it back. You shouldn't bring anything back from there, Lugh warned us not to.'

'It was a mistake,' said Hal. 'But when we got back last time, we cut the tree down and dug out its roots. This root is going to be our Yule Log. We'd thought we'd start burning it while you're here.'

'Wow,' said Ben, as he inspected it. 'It's awfully big. How long had the tree been growing?'

'Not long at all,' said Hal.

'Magic, of course,' said Gilly.

'Are you sure you should burn it?' asked Ben.

'It's only the root,' said Hal confidently. 'And it's been drying out by the side of the stove in the kitchen. No magical manifestations, so it'll be all right.'

'What's your news, Ben?' said Gilly, winning the fight with Hal for the best place on the sofa.

'Well,' said Ben. 'It's like this. You know my dad vanished a while back?'

'Yes.'

'He'd done it before.' This was the painful bit; Ben hated his dad for running out on them, but he tried to remember the good things about him as well. This wasn't a good thing.

'What, run out on you?'

'No. Run out on someone else. He was married before, and he left his wife. Not long after they'd got married. My mum says his first wife found my dad really strange, and had a kind of nervous breakdown. She told him to go, said she'd go mad if he stayed.'

'Sounds sad,' said Gilly, slipping on to her knees in front of the fireplace and jostling the smouldering log vigorously with the poker.

'Leave it *be*,' said Hal. 'It's doing okay.'

'I don't really understand it,' said Ben. 'Anyway, my

mum knew he'd been married before, although she never told me. Then just a few days ago, she got a letter. That's what made her tell me about it.'

'What letter?'

'It was from my father's ex. Saying that she had married again, and her daughter and this other chap she'd married didn't get on at all, and it was time that my father took some responsibility for his daughter.'

'*His* daughter?' Gilly was sitting bolt upright on the sofa, fascinated.

'She'd had a baby after Dad left. He never knew, and she never said. So it was a real shock for my mum. And a shock for me, because suddenly, I'd got a sister. And one who might turn up on the doorstep.'

'Not very likely now that your pa's done a bunk,' said Hal. 'Wouldn't be much point.'

'Mum feels sorry for her. Says it's rotten when you don't get on with a step-parent. She feels that we ought to see if she wants to live with us.'

'Bit of a squash, wouldn't it be?'

'Mum says we'd manage.'

'Are you sure she's your sister? She might be trying it on.'

'Her mum sent a photo,' said Ben. 'She looks just like my dad. And her hair's red, the same colour as mine and Dad's.'

'Pretty conclusive,' said Hal with a grin, looking at Ben's fiery head.

'I think you're very lucky,' said Gilly, getting up from the sofa, determined to do further battle with the fire. 'I think having a long-lost sister turn up is really exciting.'

'Not so much long-lost as unknown,' pointed out Hal, who had a precise mind. 'Do leave that alone, Gilly. It's all set up to burn nice and slowly, it doesn't need you rattling it about with the poker.'

'What's the use of a fire with no glow and no crackling flames?' said Gilly. 'Let's put another fire-lighter under it, and really get it going.'

'That was a really stupid idea,' said Hal a few minutes later. 'Look at all the smoke.'

Gilly was coughing violently. Ben had pulled his sweatshirt up to cover his mouth and nose.

'I think we'd better open a window,' he said indistinctly.

'Can't see the window,' said Hal.

'Can't see anything,' said Gilly.

'It's like being in a black cloud of smoky mist,' said Ben.

'Oh, no,' said Hal.

Forty

'IT'S HOPELESS, THEN,' SAID SCARLET. 'THERE'S no way we can get to him, or get him out.'

'Yes, there is,' said Ivar. 'Let Uthar capture you, then he'll threaten Merleon and get him to come out that way.'

'I've told you, I'm not his daughter. He'll just look through that marbled glass, pull a few faces and go back to whatever it is he does all day.'

Mab wasn't wasting time on fancies like these. 'Ivar, stop it,' she said. 'Mischief-making, like all your kind. Of course we aren't going to let Scarlet be caught by Uthar, what a bad idea.'

'What are we going to do then?' said Pebin.

'Find the Dewstone,' said Mab at once.

Ivar laughed, long and hard. Scarlet sat and gazed at the dome; Pebin was startled. 'Just like that?' he said. 'It's not very likely. Why, those Otherworlders who found it before had a terrible time over it. Didn't one of them have to travel out of time to where the dragons live?'

'Yes, but that was then.'

'Where is it now? It was lost again, so people said.'

'It lies at the bottom of the Spellbound Gorge,' said Ivar. 'Not even we demigods could get it from there.'

'Too deep,' agreed Pebin, picturing it in his mind's eye.

'Not that,' said Ivar. 'Only Merleon or his descendants can reclaim the Dewstone. Someone else can only have it if it's given to them.'

'Right, Scarlet,' said Mab. 'On your feet. Pebin, draw us a map. You can do it on the rock over there.'

'Map?'

'Of how we get to the Spellbound Gorge. How long will it take?'

Pebin searched in his mind. 'It isn't far from here at all.'

Mab looked up at the sky. 'Just as well, because those clouds and those winds bode no good to us or the Tuans or the Walled City. The balance is being strained, anybody can see that.'

Scarlet was inclined to argue. 'Look, we've found Merleon. That means I should be able to go home.'

'What, and leave us here in this peril?' Pebin was shocked.

'It's your peril.'

'If Merleon's your father . . .'

'Which he isn't.'

'Okay, prove it. If you can pick up the Dewstone, then you're his daughter. If you can't, you aren't, and three countries tumble into anarchy, maybe even come to an end.'

'Besides,' said Mab, 'I don't think the time is come for you to return to your world. There are no doorways or entrances of any kind here. No fords, no mist, none of the usual signs. I think you have some time still left with us.'

Ivar yawned. 'Come,' he said. 'Let's see this little drama played out to its end. Then I, at least, can return home, and I shall be glad to get back to a normal life in pleasant surroundings.'

'Lucky old you,' said Pebin, thinking of his home in the Walled City, no doubt bolted and shuttered against a foe and a fate that no locks or bars would protect them from.

'Oh, all right,' said Scarlet ungraciously. 'I'm really fed up with this. Do this, do that, and then . . . just one more thing, and then . . . Only then never comes.'

'This way,' said Mab.

'Will those forest people still follow us?'

'Bound to,' said Mab.

'We'll scout for you,' said the arpad, who'd been quietly doing a spot of feather-grooming. 'As long as the weather doesn't get much worse.'

Ivar climbed back up to the top of the hill.

'Is their way still blocked?' asked Pebin.

'Only a matter of time, now,' said Ivar. 'We'd better get going.'

The arpad had done a preliminary circle round, and now landed in a swirl of wings and fright. 'Not just the forest-dwellers,' said Beak One.

'No, indeed,' said Two. 'Uthar with a troop of men are behind them.'

'And Requin's there as well.'

'What a merry outing,' said Scarlet, as they set off down the hill at a cracking pace.

Forty-One

SOON AFTER THAT, REQUIN CAUGHT UP WITH Uthar. 'They've gone in a new direction,' he said.

'How do you know?' asked Uthar.

Requin looked at him with scorn. 'It is my business to know.'

'Are they lost? You said they would lead us to Merleon.'

'They have found him, or at least, they have found the place of his imprisonment.'

'Then what are we waiting for?'

'Go ahead,' said Requin. 'Waste your time prowling about his glass prison, much good it will do you.'

'If the girl is there, then my task is done.'

'Only she isn't. She isn't there any more.'

'Where is she?'

A familiar voice came from a pathway which ran slightly above them. 'She's heading for the Spellbound Gorge.'

Uthar stared up in astonishment. 'Erica!' he said. 'And Culun. Why are you here?'

'To warn you that the Red One and those two tedious Otherworlders have come through into our world again. They are at the Spellbound Gorge, a spy has just brought me the news.'

'The Dewstone,' cried Uthar, his face darkening with

joy. 'I shall have it all, Merleon, the Dewstone and unimaginable power.'

He turned to Requin. 'Which is the swiftest way to the Spellbound Gorge from here? Quick, man, speak up.'

'Man? Uthar, I am not one of your slaves or erstwhile colleagues.'

'Erstwhile is what you will be if you don't tell me.' Uthar took a threatening step forward. 'I know about your magic, but you aren't in your chamber now, you don't have the world at your beckoning. Not with the balance in turmoil as it is now. This is my hour, my triumph. Now, tell me the way.'

Requin shrugged. 'Very well. Go back and take the other turning at the fork down there. That will lead you directly to the Gorge. And Uthar . . .'

'What?'

'We magicians have an old saying.'

'Yes?'

'Don't count your chickens before they're hatched.'

'Chickens?' Uthar exploded. 'What have chickens to do with ruling a mighty empire?'

'More than you think,' muttered Requin. 'And bring a map next time.'

Forty-Two

'WHERE ARE WE?' SAID HAL.

Gilly was still coughing. 'We should have known better than to burn that root,' she said.

'I don't think it would have made any difference,' said Hal, philosophical now. 'If it hadn't been that, it would have been something else. The first time we came through we were wandering round a museum, and the next time we got caught up in a mist at the bottom of the garden. It just happens.'

'Well, I wish it wouldn't,' said Gilly, looking around. 'I think we've arrived just before some kind of storm. The air feels hot and heavy, and look at that sky!'

Hal looked, and wished he hadn't. He had never seen anything so threatening and ominous. He shivered, despite the heat. 'Where's Ben?'

'Ben! BEN!'

Hal and Gilly were in a dense green glade, with thick grass underfoot. Trees with gnarled and twisted trunks grew round the edge of the circular patch of grass, their grotesque shadows flicking backwards and forwards in the strong wind.

'Not here,' said Hal.

'Where then?'

'Who knows,' said Hal.

'He can't be far, we came through together.'

'In this place, who knows?' said Hal. 'He may not be

far away; he wouldn't hear us shouting, not with these winds and the noise those trees are making.'

'There's what looks like a way through the trees over there,' said Gilly.

Two minutes' walk, and they both knew where they were.

'The Spellbound Gorge,' said Hal. 'Don't look down, you'll get dizzy.' He went closer to the edge.

'Hal,' shrieked Gilly.

'Just looking. I can see Ben, he's halfway down, on a ledge. Bother it, I can't see him getting down from there in a hurry. Or up. Ben!' he shouted.

Far below, Ben looked up, a tiny figure, and waved. He seemed to be pointing at something down at the bottom of the gorge. Hal strained his eyes to see what it was. Animals? People?

Then a beam of sunlight from between the raging clouds lit up the figures below. Hal stared down into the gorge. A very tall man, with a glow about him, a demigod, by the look of him. A boy, and a more familiar figure. 'Mab,' he shouted. Then he saw the fourth person move out from behind the others.

'That hair,' said Hal. 'Just look at that hair. Exactly the same as Ben's.'

Ben, being closer, could see more clearly. It was the sister he had seen in his dreams. She was with a boy, and a woman, and a very tall man, it looked like one of those demigods he'd met up with last time he was here.

They were looking for something, that was obvious. For what?

Ben didn't even have to ask himself. He knew exactly what they were searching for, turning over large stones, running fingers and feet through long grass, going

—— 172 ——

down to the river, now a foaming torrent, which ran along the floor of the gorge.

My Dewstone, thought Ben, with a surge of possessive anger which startled him with its strength. They shan't have it, it's mine, or if not mine, nobody's. I threw it into the gorge so that it would be lost, not so that a party of trippers should find it.

His rage died as swiftly as it had flared. At that moment the red-headed one looked up. She saw Ben, and stood stock still, staring.

She stared and stared.

Ben summoned all his breath, and bellowed into the wind. 'CAN YOU HEAR ME?'

She nodded, and made a thumbs-up gesture.

'YOU'RE LOOKING IN THE WRONG PLACE. GO DOWNSTREAM, TO THAT ROCK SHAPED LIKE A BOOT.'

'BO-O-OT?' The word wafted back to him.

'YES. WHAT YOU ARE LOOKING FOR IS THERE.'

'Voice of the Gods?' remarked Ivar, who had been listening with astonishment. 'Surely a boy couldn't shout so loudly.'

'It's amazing what you can do when you have to,' said Mab. 'That's the Red One, and further up, near the top, are Hal and Gilly. The ones who cut off Ril's head,' she reminded him.

'And buried it in time, so that it joined up with his body again. I've a bone to pick with them.' He winced. 'Not a bone, maybe, but I blame them for all my troubles.'

'Nonsense, it was those Gods, it always is. Now, get a move on, we can't leave Scarlet on her own.'

Pebin was with Scarlet, and the two of them had

reached the boot stone, and were casting around it in a doubtful way.

'Do you know what this Dewstone looks like?' Scarlet asked.

Pebin shook his head. 'Never seen it, well, practically nobody has. It can't be very big, though, because the Red One had it in his pocket.'

Scarlet looked about her in dismay. Scattered around the base of the boot stone were hundreds and hundreds of roundish stones, each slightly bigger than a tennis ball, all able to be fitted into a pocket.

'Is it one of these?'

Mab made her favourite tsk-ing noise. 'Dear, oh dear. Scarlet, you'll never find it by looking.'

'I won't find it anyway,' said Scarlet, who was still sure that she and the Dewstone would have nothing to do with each other.

'Let the Dewstone itself guide you,' said Mab. 'Shut your eyes, and walk among the stones. Then pick up the one that calls you.'

'A stone? Call me? Are you crazy?'

'Course she is,' said Pebin. 'All witches are, it goes with the job. It's good practice, though, that's what my parents would tell you to do.'

'Oh, what a waste of time this is,' said Scarlet. 'All that'll happen is that I'll trip over the first stone and fall flat on my face.'

'You won't,' said Pebin.

She didn't.

Eyes screwed shut, Scarlet walked through the stones like a cat. How funny, she thought. I can see them all, quite clearly, even with my eyes shut. And they're all pink and grey, except for that one, there, which is glowing like a rainbow. That's the one I want.

She bent down and picked it up, her eyes flying open

—— 174 ——

as it settled in her hand, almost burning her with its heat. It flared to a brilliant blue colour and then settled back into looking like any other stone.

'It isn't, though,' said Scarlet, fingering the markings on its surface. She looked up to where Ben was standing on his ledge and waved the stone triumphantly in the air.

The single word 'GREAT' floated down to her.

'What did he say?' asked Pebin, straining to catch Ben's other words.

'NOW USE IT,' shouted Ben.

Forty-Three

'I THINK NOT,' SAID A GRAVELLY VOICE.

Hal and Ben looked down from their respective perches, helplessly watching Uthar and his troop advancing down the gorge.

'That's torn it,' said Hal, as he noticed Erica, Culun and a team from Uthar's force moving into position at the other end of the gorge. Would Scarlet realize the power she held in her hand? Would she use the strength of the Dewstone to send Uthar and Erica and all of them out of time – if she so wished?

Scarlet tried. She held the Dewstone at arm's length, willing it, as she had the thoughtball, to do something to Uthar and his mob.

Uthar's laugh rang mockingly through the gorge.

'No good, redhead. Just come quietly, hand over the Dewstone like a good girl. No point trying anything, because the Dewstone has no power, here in the Spellbound Gorge.'

Mab looked at Ivar. 'True?' she mouthed.

'Yes,' said Ivar, quite unconcerned. 'You should know that. It's why the gorge is called spellbound. All spells are bound, they don't work. It includes the Dewstone, because the binding put on this gorge and on the river was made by the old magic and the Gods. At a time when they were in cahoots over this and that. Relationships were strained as time went on, but they never changed what was done here.'

'So the Dewstone has no power?'

'Not unless she can get herself and it out of the gorge. Not very likely with that laughing jackass standing there, and his ill-natured daughter lurking down that way. No, she hasn't a hope.'

'She has.'

The cool voice cut across Uthar's exclamations of glee as he advanced triumphantly on Scarlet. 'The Dewstone, the Dewstone. Mine, all mine!'

Scarlet stared at the figure standing behind Uthar's men. Requin looked as crafty and immaculate as ever, out here in the copper light, with the clouds swirling closer and closer to the ground.

'Since you are a descendant of the Old Kings, you can swim in the river. It was made to flow by the old magic, and it will guard its own.'

'No,' shouted Pebin. 'Don't believe him, Scarlet. Nobody trusts Requin, don't do it.'

'Fool,' said Requin. 'Do you think I want Vemoria to rule us all under this hobgoblin here?'

'Hobgoblin?' said Uthar, momentarily distracted.

'THE RIVER, JUMP IN THE RIVER. IT'S WHAT I WOULD DO.'

And who are you? thought Scarlet, her heart thumping as she looked round for a way out. Give up the Dewstone? Never.

'I can't swim,' she said, and leapt into the raging torrent.

The water rose in terrifying waves and seethed and boiled around the spot where she had jumped. Flecks of foam were tossed in the air and fell back to slither over the violent surface of the water. Overhead, there was a gigantic crack of thunder.

Of Scarlet, there was no sign.

Forty-Four

HAL LEANED OVER AS FAR AS HE DARED. 'BEN,' he yelled. 'There's a path which leads up here. Look behind that rock there, and you'll see it.'

Ben was up the precipitous path like a mountain goat.

'That was terrible,' said Gilly. 'Was that your sister, Ben? She must have drowned. No one could survive in that river.'

Ben was having none of it. 'She's all right,' he said. 'I know it was the only thing to do, to jump into the water. I could hear the river calling out to her.'

'Siren voices, summoning sailors to their doom,' said Hal gloomily.

'Don't be so pessimistic,' said Gilly. 'If Ben heard that, then she may have survived.'

'Where does the river go?' Hal was straining his eyes to follow its course, not easy in the dim light under storm-clouded skies. 'It dives underground, and then where?'

'I don't know,' said Ben.

'So what do we do now?' said Gilly, carefully keeping a good distance from the edge; she'd had her heart in her mouth when Ben's head had appeared over the cliff top and Hal had bent over to haul him up the last few feet.

'We'll follow Uthar,' said Hal. 'He set off at such a

lick when Ben's sister went, that he must have been up to something.'

'Wasn't that Mab down there?' said Gilly as they set off on down the slope which led away from the gorge.

'It looked like it.'

'Maybe we'll meet up with her.'

'Maybe sooner than you think,' said a growly voice.

They whirled round to see a black panther standing behind them. Ben tensed with fear, bunching his fists to run.

'Hold on,' said Hal. 'Mab?'

'Ha, had you there for a moment,' said Mab, changing back into her normal shape, much to Ben's relief. 'So this is the Red One, is it?' she said to Ben. 'That was your sister down there, cutting those capers.'

'Mab, do you think she drowned? She shouted that she couldn't swim.'

'Drowned? Oh, I don't think so. The old magic looks after its own. Meanwhile, we'd better get along. Uthar's up to some wickedness, you may be sure; he's heading back to Merleon's dome.'

'Merleon's dome?'

'I'll tell you about it as we go,' said Mab. 'Hurry up, no time to lose.'

Uthar was already at the dome, prowling round the outside like a predatory animal. 'Merleon,' he shouted. 'I have your daughter held captive.'

Silence.

'Come out,' Uthar shouted. 'Come out and save her.'

'If you can,' said Erica, taunting the man who was just visible through the glass. 'If you have any powers left, come out and get your daughter. Unleash the wild magic, set her free. Look,' she went on, holding up

— 179 —

some strands of hair. 'Recognize the colour? She's your daughter all right.'

Mab and her group had joined Pebin and Ivar, who were watching from behind some trees which over-looked the dome.

'We must tell him it isn't true,' whispered Pebin. 'Where did Erica get that hair from?'

'There was some caught in a branch,' said Ivar. 'I saw her grab it, the cunning creature.'

'We can't say or do anything,' said Mab. 'Uthar would simply send his troops to deal with us. We wouldn't have a hope. At least I would, because I could turn myself into a cuckoo or something. And Ivar would give a good account of himself; but it won't do, there are too many of them. And for all we know, those forest-dwellers may still be around.'

'No,' said Pebin. 'They've gone, I'm sure they have. Requin must have sent them home.'

'If only we knew what had happened to Scarlet,' said Ben, crouching down beside Pebin.

'I can tell you where the river goes,' said Pebin. 'We did it in geography, because it's one of the rivers of the Gods.'

'Where?'

Pebin shut his eyes, and lines began to appear etched in the grass underfoot.

'That's the Spellbound Gorge,' said Mab. 'And that's where she went underground.'

'It meanders all over the place,' said Hal, frowning. 'Which way did we come?'

'Look,' said Gilly. 'That must be an underground lake. And there are lots of stream running out of it, apart from the main river, which is heading for the sea. One of them may be the stream trickling by the dome down there. The direction would be right.'

The others looked at the map in silence, except for Pebin, who was beginning to get a headache and wanted to open his eyes. 'I can't hold it,' he said, and the grass shimmered back into place. 'Any good?' he said, blinking and rubbing the back of his head.

'Scarlet's ended up in an underground lake,' said Mab. 'This stream leads out of it. Perhaps she'll pick on the right one, to come out from underground.'

'A one-in-fourteen chance. If she's still alive,' said Hal.

'How come?'

'There were fourteen streams; I counted them.'

Forty-Five

SCARLET, BATTERED AND WITH ALL THE BREATH knocked out of her, floated across the sluggish surface of the lake. She could hear the water booming through the underground caves, but in here it was completely calm. Then a ripple from the centre of the lake caught her and pushed her out of the water on to a beach.

Some beach, thought Scarlet, rolling over and throwing up all the water she had swallowed. Disgusting taste it had. The sand beneath her was chilly and black, with tiny flints of crystal mixed in with the black dust.

Like some vast coal bunker, Scarlet thought.

It seemed an age before she felt strong enough to sit up, and then to get unsteadily to her feet. Her right hand ached with the effort of holding the Dewstone, but she had it still. Now it glowed, and began to feel warm as it had when she first picked it up.

'What next, stone?' she asked it.

'There,' cried Gilly out loud, forgetting the need for caution. 'She's there.'

The others shushed her, but not before a sharp word from Uthar sent ten of his troop wheeling off and heading towards the part of the hill where Gilly and the others were watching.

'Now look what you've done,' said Hal crossly. 'We'll have to move.'

'No, look,' said Gilly. 'It's Scarlet. Over there, between those trees.'

Gilly's eyes were very sharp, and at first the others couldn't see what she had seen. Then Scarlet came into the open, walking slowly alongside the stream.

Uthar saw her, too.

'Give me the Dewstone,' he yelled, heedless of what Erica and Culun were saying to him.

'Dad, no go. It's too late.'

'My lord, the Dewstone will have its full power here.'

'We have to go,' said Erica, tugging at her father's sleeve. 'Quickly, before she can use the stone.'

Uthar shook his arm free. 'I will have it,' he shouted.

'No,' said Scarlet, pointing the stone in his direction. 'Be bound, man of darkness. Stay still until I bid you. And you, and all of you.'

'How idiotic they look,' said Pebin, slithering down the hillside to join Scarlet. 'Hey, you did it, you did it.'

'Don't they look silly?' said Scarlet. 'Like a bunch of kids playing statues.' She wasn't looking at Pebin, but over his shoulder at Ben.

'Hi,' she said at last. 'You must be my brother.'

'Yes,' said Ben.

'How about we go rescue our father?'

'Can we?'

'This Dewstone,' said Scarlet, 'can do anything.'

Merleon was stunned by his unexpected freedom; a freedom not paid for by letting loose the old magic.

He glowered at Requin, an ancient foe, who had joined them in the valley, and now swept an elegant bow to Merleon. 'Congratulations on your freedom,' he said.

'Requin, you old fox, you put me in there.'

'Only under orders, I assure you it hurt me as much as it did you.'

'A likely story,' said Merleon, with a twisted smile. 'I could have broken out whenever I wanted to.'

Requin smiled his cold smile. 'You didn't, though,' he pointed out. 'I knew you wouldn't, not with what was at stake.'

Merleon laughed. He had an arm round Scarlet and Ben, and was looking from one to the other with amazement. 'Ben, you're so tall, I wouldn't have recognized you. And you're the daughter I never knew I had.'

Scarlet nodded.

'Time we got to know each other, then.'

Requin gave a polite cough. 'So sorry to interrupt this touching family reunion, but something has to be done about Uthar and his daughter and the rest of them.'

'Leave them there,' said Scarlet.

'Not a good idea,' said Requin, affronted. 'They can't be left littering up the valley, this isn't a village green, you know.'

'What do you suggest then?' said Merleon.

'It depends on what you are planning to do.'

'Take that greedy look out of your eyes, Requin. The magic of the Old Kings is finished. I'm going back to the Otherworld, to pick up the life I left behind there. With Ben and Scarlet, and my wife.'

'Just so,' said Requin, hiding his disappointment with a suave smile. 'In that case, I think Uthar must go.'

'Go where?' said Scarlet.

'Out of time,' said Merleon. 'Very well. But not his daughter.'

'Send her back across the black bar,' advised Mab.

'What's that?' asked Gilly.

'We draw a bar, and once Erica has crossed back into her world over it, she can never come back here.'

'Bit hard on our world,' muttered Hal.

'Where is this bar?' said Gilly.

'Here,' said Mab, and, as she walked very precisely along a strip of grass, it turned black behind her and shone like marble.

'I suggest that Hal and I take Erica across,' said Gilly.

'Good idea,' said Hal.

'Culun?' asked Requin.

'Send him back to Vemoria. He can restore the Twelve, and take Uthar's place in the council. Let him learn a lesson from what Uthar has done.'

'And I'm going to deliver Pebin back to his family in the Walled City,' said Mab.

'Then I shall go back to south Tuan, and to my witchy duties.'

'We'd better go soon,' said Pebin, who didn't want to see Uthar sent out of time; it sounded very unpleasant. He looked up into the sky. 'And the arpad can come with us, there she is. It's going to rain, I think.'

'No,' said Requin. 'The clouds are lifting, and the fountains will be running in the Walled City by the time you get home. I'll have a word with your teachers, I think you'd better come and study with me.'

'In the castle?' Pebin looked very alarmed. 'Oh, no, thank you. I mean, I'm very honoured, but I would not be any use, not at your level. I'm hopeless at my lessons, everyone says so.'

'You have the makings of a great magician,' said Requin. 'I should know, being one myself.'

He turned to Merleon. 'It is time.'

Scarlet lifted the Dewstone, and Uthar came out of his frozen stance. He opened his mouth, but before he could say anything, Merleon pointed at him, and with a crack like a squib going off, he vanished. Hal and Gilly ran towards Erica and grabbed her as she came back to life. Waving their goodbyes, they jumped with her over the bar and back into the Otherworld.

'Goodbye, Mab,' said Scarlet, giving her a hug. 'Goodbye, bendy-man.'

'Bendy-man! Really,' said Ivar, affronted.

'We'll see you soon,' said Mab.

'Not if I have anything to do with it,' said Merleon grimly, as a mist started to roll towards them from the stream.

'They'll decide for themselves,' said Mab. 'Just as you did. Take care of the Dewstone, Merleon. Keep it in the Otherworld, where it can't do any mischief.'

'I will,' said Merleon, as the mist swallowed the three of them up, and they disappeared from sight and from that world.

THE TALKING HEAD

'I don't make a habit of carrying anybody's head around. It's uncivilised.'

But Gilly and Hal, who inadvertently step through an arch and into a land outside time and space have to do exactly that. The head has red curls, green eyes and a difficult personality, and is accompanied by a tiresome talking raven. To get back to their own world, and to stop the Vemorians invading Tuan, they have to bury the head in the appointed place before the next full moon – and the head is distinctly unhelpful.

THE DEWSTONE QUEST

'It's not the sort of thing you learn at school, making dragons laugh.'

When Ben vanishes into the fog, he finds himself in the strange world his friends Hal and Gilly have visited once before, called to fulfil a prophecy and find the Dewstone. But a lot of unpleasant people want to use the stone for their own ends – including the malicious Numens and foul cousin Erica.

With the dubious help of a spy, a Dollop, a touchy dragon and an arrogant Immortal, among others, Hal and Gilly race to find Ben before his enemies do. But even if they succeed, Ben still has to make the right decision . . .